LEGEND OF THE ICE DEMON

ARCANE MAGE KOLOS
BOOK I

by Joel Poe

Copyright © 2023 by Joel Poe.

All rights reserved. No portion of this book may be reproduced, stored in a retrieval system, or transmitted in any form or by any means--electronic, mechanical, photocopy, recording, scanning, or other- -except for brief quotations in critical reviews or articles, without the prior written permission of the publisher or author.

This book is copyright protected and registered by the United States Copyright Office

Library of Congress.

Publishers note: This is a work of fiction. Names, characters, places, and incidents are either products of the author's imagination or used fictitiously. All characters are fictional, and any similarity to people living or dead is purely coincidental.

Copyright © 2023 Joel Poe

All rights reserved.

www.joelpoe.com

CONTENTS

LEGEND OF THE ICE DEMON 1

CONTENTS 2

PROLOGUE 6

CHAPTER 1 12

CHAPTER 2 18

CHAPTER 3 23

CHAPTER 4 29

CHAPTER 5 34

CHAPTER 6 38

CHAPTER 7 42

CHAPTER 8 46

CHAPTER 9 50

CHAPTER 10 53

CHAPTER 11 57

CHAPTER 12 61

CHAPTER 13 65

CHAPTER 14 69

CHAPTER 15 73

CHAPTER 16 78

CHAPTER 17 83

- **CHAPTER 18** 87
- **CHAPTER 19** 91
- **CHAPTER 20** 96
- **CHAPTER 21** 101
- **CHAPTER 22** 105
- **CHAPTER 23** 109
- **CHAPTER 24** 113
- **CHAPTER 25** 119
- **CHAPTER 26** 124
- **CHAPTER 27** 129
- **CHAPTER 28** 134
- **CHAPTER 29** 141
- **CHAPTER 30** 147
- **CHAPTER 31** 152
- **CHAPTER 32** 157
- **CHAPTER 33** 163
- **CHAPTER 34** 170
- **CHAPTER 35** 175
- **CHAPTER 36** 180
- **CHAPTER 37** 184
- **CHAPTER 38** 188
- **CHAPTER 39** 193

CHAPTER 40	198
CHAPTER 41	204
CHAPTER 42	209
CHAPTER 43	214
CHAPTER 44	220
CHAPTER 45	227
CHAPTER 46	234
EPILOGUE	238

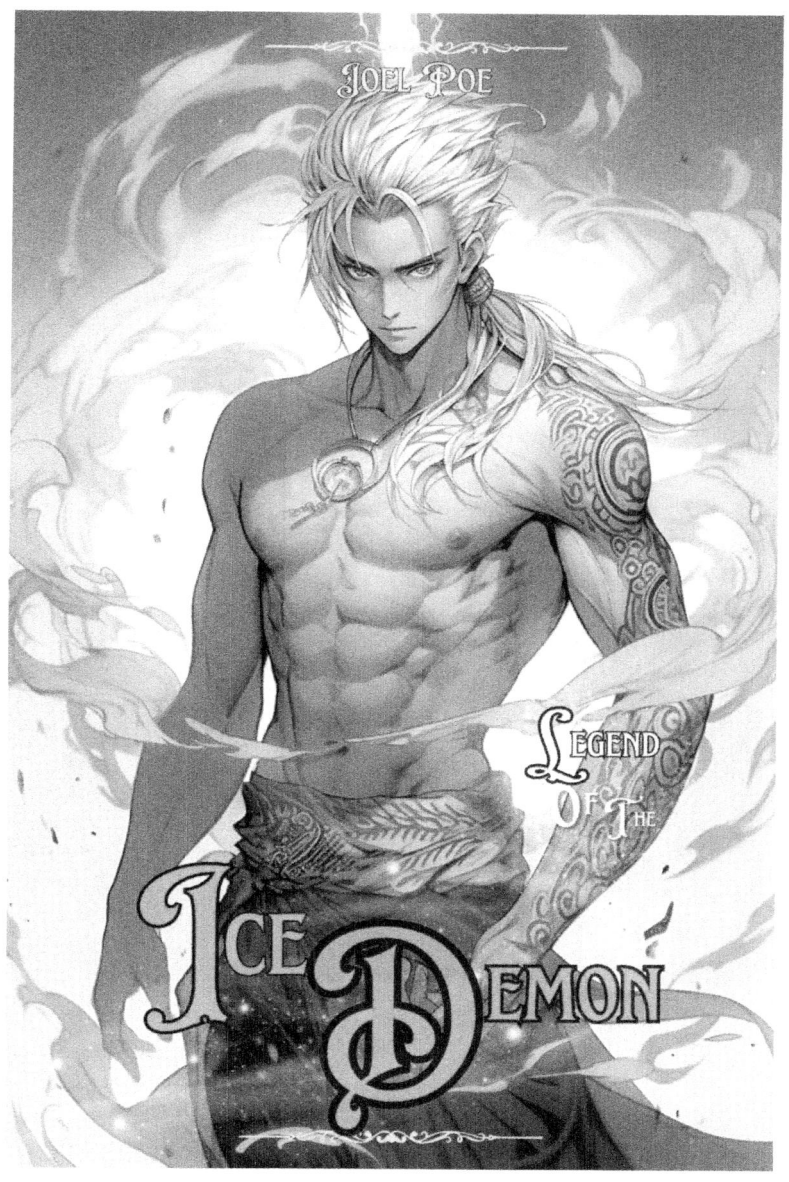

Prologue

I was born a slave, property of the Baron of Daileem. From a young age, I was taught to obey, to bend to the will of my master. That's all I knew, that's all I was... until the day he discovered my magic. Suddenly, I was worth more than the dirt beneath his feet. I became his precious golden goose, a circus freak paraded around for the amusement of others. I was a spectacle, performing cheap tricks for the masses who paid to watch me. The humiliation of it still makes my cheeks burn, even after all these years.

But I didn't let my circumstances define me. No, I planned my escape. I remember it like it was yesterday, the metallic taste of revenge on my tongue. The night I decided to fight back, to reclaim my freedom. I can still feel the coolness of the ice shard I formed from his own saliva. The

moment I plunged it into his throat...
I'd had enough. Enough of his
torment, his laughter, his mockery.
The hubris to think he was
untouchable. Only to end up begging
for his life as he choked in his own
blood. I made sure my face was the
last thing he saw, as he lay dying in a
pool of his own filth. I was his
property no more.

Then came the running. My heart
pounding, my breath ragged, and the
endless fear driving me forward. I ran
until I couldn't feel my legs. Until I
reached Sadrym, a place as broken
and desolate as I was. There, I lived as
an outcast, a homeless boy with
nothing to his name but his freedom.
But it was enough. I learned to
survive, to steal just enough to keep
the gnawing hunger at bay.

One day, my theft was not just of bread, but of magic. Magic I barely understood. I remember stealing from an old witch, a magical artifact that I barely remember now. All I remember is the hunger that drove me to it. The hunger that twisted my insides into knots, the hunger that made me desperate. But it was a different kind. It was hunger for power.

Then he found me. Antonius Silverhand. The Storm Fox himself. He caught me, dragged me by the ear back to the old witch, and made me return what I had stolen. I remember the shame burning in my cheeks as I stuttered out an apology. I hated him in that moment, with every fiber of my being. But instead of turning me over to the authorities, he took me in. He fed me, clothed me, and most importantly, he taught me. He showed me how to wield my magic, how to control the power that had been a curse for so long.

To this day, I don't know why he chose to help me. Perhaps he saw something in me, a spark of potential, a chance for redemption. Or perhaps he just pitied the scrappy, half-starved kid who knew nothing of the world. Whatever his reasons, Antonius Silverhand became more than a mentor to me. He became my savior, my guide, the only father figure I've ever known.

But I am not content to simply follow in his footsteps. I crave more. I crave power still, the kind of power that will etch my name in the annals of history. I don't want to live in the shadow of my master.

In the ruthless world of magic, power often comes at a price. Each battle fought; each level gained brings me closer to my destiny. I am Kolos. My name will be remembered in history as the greatest mage this world has ever seen…

I swear it.

Chapter 1

The morning dawned cool and clear, the crisp air filled with the scent of pine and damp earth. I stood in the training grounds, my heart pounding in my chest as I faced my mentor. Antonius Silverhand, the greatest mage in the history of Aelloria, was a formidable figure. His commanding presence was amplified by the raw power he effortlessly wielded. To say I was nervous would be an understatement.

"Remember, Kolos," he began, his voice calm and steady, "the art of the arcane isn't about raw power. It's about control, finesse. You must feel the flow of magic, let it guide your actions."

I nodded, focusing my attention on the energy coursing through my veins. The taste of magic was intoxicating, the sensation like a live wire sparking beneath my skin. I could feel it, the raw potential waiting to be unleashed.

With a deep breath, I thrust my hands forward, shaping the magic into a sharp, pulsing wave. It shot towards Antonius, a streak of icy blue energy.

But with a casual flick of his wrist, Antonius deflected it, his own magic forming a shimmering barrier that absorbed my attack. My heart sank as I watched my efforts dissolve into nothing.

"Again," he commanded. I could hear the strain in his voice, the hint of frustration. He was pushing me, harder than he ever had before. But no matter how hard I tried, no matter what spell I conjured, he blocked them all with ease.

My frustration was mounting, a knot of anger and disappointment in my chest. I was a mage, an apprentice of the greatest mage in history. And yet, I couldn't land a single hit. It was maddening.

"Focus, Kolos!" Antonius barked, his voice echoing across the training grounds. "You're being rash. You need to concentrate, follow the flow of the arcane."

I bit back a retort, my temper flaring. But I swallowed my pride and tried again. This time, I envisioned the magic as a river, flowing and swirling within me. I tried to channel it, to guide it with precision and finesse. But my attack fizzled out, the magic sputtering and dying in the air. I could see the disappointment in Antonius's eyes, and it stung worse than any physical blow.

With a wordless cry of frustration, I turned and punched the stone wall, the sharp pain a welcome distraction from my failure. I could hear Antonius approaching, his footsteps echoing in the quiet morning air.

"Kolos," he said gently, resting a hand on my shoulder. "You must be patient. These things take time."

I wanted to argue, to tell him that I was trying my best. But the words wouldn't come. I felt so... insignificant, like a child playing at being a mage.

"But I believe in you," he continued. His words were a balm to my wounded pride. "You have the potential, Kolos. But you must also believe in yourself."

I nodded, not trusting myself to speak. I was grateful for his faith in me, even though I felt I didn't deserve it.

"Come," he said, gesturing for me to follow. "There's something I want to show you."

Curiosity piqued, I followed Antonius as he led me away from the training grounds. As we walked, I couldn't help but wonder what he had in store for me. Despite my frustration, a spark of hope flickered in my chest. Maybe, just maybe, I would find a way to prove myself. To show Antonius, and the world, what I was truly capable of.

Chapter 2

The sound of our footsteps echoed through the stone corridors of the Magic Conservatory, a haunting rhythm in the eerie silence. As we walked, I couldn't help but feel a sense of awe. The grandeur of the conservatory was something that always amazed me. Its tall, looming towers, the vast libraries filled with ancient manuscripts, and the training grounds, it was all so...enchanting.

Finally, we reached our destination: Antonius Silverhand's headmaster's office. It was an expansive room, filled with artifacts of immense power and shelves lined with magical tomes. The room was bathed in a soft, ethereal light, the walls adorned with runes that pulsed with energy.

Antonius walked over to a massive wooden desk, his hand brushing over a leather-bound book. The moment he touched it, the book began to glow, a soft, welcoming light. It was an arcane codex, a repository of magical knowledge that had been passed down through generations of mages.

"Kolos," Antonius began, his voice filled with an emotion I couldn't quite place. It was a mixture of pride and hope, tinged with a hint of sadness. "This...is my arcane codex. It contains all my magical knowledge, every spell and incantation, every runic marking."

He turned to look at me, his eyes filled with sincerity. "And I want you to have it."

The words hung in the air, their weight settling on me like a heavy cloak. This was a significant moment, a turning point. The arcane codex was not just a book. It was a testament of Antonius's faith in me.

"I...I don't know what to say," I stuttered, surprised by the suddenness of the gift. "I don't think I deserve..."

"Nonsense," Antonius interrupted, a warm smile playing on his lips. "If you weren't deserving, the codex wouldn't have accepted you."

As if on cue, the codex flew from Antonius's hands, hovering in front of me. Its pages fluttered open, revealing infinite pages of spells, incantations, and arcane knowledge. A sense of awe filled me as I reached out, my fingers brushing over the ancient pages. The book felt alive, its energy pulsating in time with my heartbeat.

"Thank you, Antonius," I said, the words barely more than a whisper. The enormity of the gift was slowly sinking in. The old man merely nodded, the corners of his eyes crinkling as he smiled.

With the codex following me like a loyal pet, I left the office and made my way to my quarters. As I walked, I couldn't help but feel a sense of anticipation, a thrill of excitement coursing through my veins. The codex was not just a gift. It was a challenge, a beacon guiding me towards my destiny.

Chapter 3

The moon hung high in the night sky, a solitary orb casting long shadows across the landscape. As the rest of the conservatory slept, I was wide awake in my quarters, the arcane codex floating in front of me. The codex was a wealth of knowledge, an unending stream of magical wisdom that I was struggling to comprehend.

My dormitory was filled with the soft glow of the codex, the light flickering with each page that turned. The room was otherwise dark, the quiet only broken by the rustle of parchment and my occasional sighs of frustration.

I had been attempting to master some of Antonius's spells, but it was proving to be more challenging than I had anticipated. Some spells fizzled out before they could even form, while others went awry, leaving small patches of frost on my wooden desk or singeing the edges of my bedspread. A few I managed to cast correctly, but they were basic spells, nothing like the complex incantations that Antonius seemed to perform with ease.

In my frustration, I waved the codex away. "You're useless," I muttered, rubbing at my eyes, tired and irritated. The codex paused, floating motionless in the air, before drifting back towards me. It opened to a new page, one that looked different from the rest. It was handwritten, the ink faded with age, and I recognized Antonius's neat script.

Intrigued, I leaned forward, my annoyance forgotten. "So, you want me to read this?" I asked the codex. In response, the book flickered, a warm, encouraging glow. "Very well," I conceded, a small smile playing on my lips.

And so, I began to read. The entry was indeed a journal of sorts, Antonius's personal musings and reflections on his magical journey. It was not a set of instructions or a series of spells, but rather, a guide on how to approach magic with respect, patience, and humility.

I read about Antonius's struggles, his failures, and his triumphs. I read about the importance of understanding the true nature of magic, not just as a tool or weapon, but as a living, breathing entity to be nurtured and respected. I read about the importance of patience, of perseverance, and above all, of believing in oneself.

But as I read, I also came across something I don't think I was meant to find. A chapter named *Of Magic Amplification and the Storm Fox.*

"Magic amplification?" I muttered to myself, "now I'm interested…".

The dormitory had been cold and quiet, the perfect environment for sleep. But sleep was the furthest thing from my mind. Instead, I was hunched over the arcane codex, the flickering candlelight casting an eerie glow over its ancient pages. Antonius' handwriting, intricate and elegant, had weaved a tale that had held me captive.

As I read, I was drawn into a story that felt oddly familiar, a mirror of my own burning desire for more arcane power. It was Antonius' story, but it could have just as easily been mine.

He had written about his relentless search for the legendary Storm Fox, a kindred arcane spirit that was believed to amplify a mage's power a hundredfold. It was a creature of myth, dismissed as a fairy tale by most. But Antonius had believed in it.

He had searched for it, dedicating his life to uncovering its existence.

He had journeyed through Aelloria, the last sanctuary of the mythical arcane creatures that have since vanished, hunted to extinction, or died out. But his journey hadn't been in vain. Against all odds, he had found it - the Storm Fox, the last of Alloria's mythical creatures.

Chapter 4

I had been on the brink of learning what happened after Antonius found the legendary Storm Fox when the codex abruptly closed. It was as if a hidden force had intervened, cutting me off from Antonius' tale. I tried to pry it open, but the book was as unyielding as a locked vault.

"Open," I had commanded, my voice echoing in the empty dormitory. But the codex didn't budge. I felt a surge of frustration, mixed with a nagging sense of curiosity. What was so secret about this part of Antonius' journey that it needed to be locked away?

The realization had hit me like a slap in the face. A spell. The codex was under a spell, one that I hadn't sensed before. I could feel Antonius' magical imprint all over it, a signature as unique as a fingerprint.

It was a powerful enchantment, one designed to keep prying eyes away. But I was not just any prying eyes. I was a mage in training, eager to understand the arcane secrets that Antonius had discovered.

I spent hours trying to break the spell, poring over every incantation and counter-spell I knew. But the seal held firm, refusing to yield to my attempts. It was like trying to crack open a nut with a feather.

My frustration gave way to determination. If the codex wouldn't reveal its secrets, then I would have to ask Antonius himself. He was the only one who could shed light on what happened after he found the Storm Fox.

I had made up my mind. I was going to find Antonius and ask him. I didn't know how he would react, but I was willing to take the risk.

With that thought in mind, I had risen from my chair, leaving the stubborn codex behind on my desk. The dormitory was quiet, the only sound the soft rustling of the wind outside. I had opened the door and stepped out into the hallway, the dim light from the moon casting long shadows.

As I made my way towards the headmaster's quarters, the codex's secrets loomed in my mind. The story it held, Antonius' encounter with the Storm Fox, felt like a missing piece of a puzzle. A puzzle I was determined to solve.

The night was quiet, the rest of the academy asleep. The only sound was the soft crunch of my footsteps against the gravel. I had no idea what the morning would bring, but I knew one thing for certain. I was about to

face my mentor, ready to uncover the
truth hidden within the arcane codex.

Chapter 5

I arrived at Antonius' quarters, the grandiose doors towering above me. They were embellished with intricate carvings of mythical creatures and arcane symbols, a testament to Antonius' status and power. Gathering my courage, I rapped on the door loudly, my knuckles echoing against the solid wood.

Minutes passed, but it felt like hours. Finally, I heard footsteps approach from the other side. The door creaked open to reveal a bleary-eyed Antonius. He looked at me in surprise, his usual composed demeanor replaced by one of confusion and annoyance.

"What is the meaning of this, Kolos?" Antonius demanded, his voice a rumble in the quiet night.

I didn't waste any time. My questions came out in a rush, each one more accusatory than the last. "Did you kill it? What happened after you found the fox? Is this why they call you the Storm Fox? Do you keep it prisoner?"

Antonius held up a hand, silencing me. He looked at me for a moment before his gaze shifted to the floating codex that had followed me. His eyes narrowed as he observed the codex, which flickered in what seemed like a shrug.

"So that's what this is about…" Antonius murmured, rubbing his forehead. "You weren't supposed to read those pages, Kolos."

His tone was stern, yet there was a hint of resignation in his voice. I could tell he was weighing his options, deciding whether to reveal his secrets or keep them hidden.

After a long moment of silence, Antonius sighed heavily. "Very well," he conceded, stepping aside to let me in. "Come in. I'll tell you everything you want to know."

Chapter 6

I followed Antonius into his office, the space larger and more grandiose than I ever could have imagined. An arcane orb of light flickered into existence at Antonius' command, casting shadows that danced across the room as it hovered and followed us. The walls were adorned with oil paintings, portraits of Antonius' predecessors, each gaze heavy with history and knowledge.

"Keep up, Kolos," Antonius urged, snapping me out of my awe as I slowed to examine the magical artifacts and gadgets that populated the room. His voice echoed in the cavernous office, a reminder that we were here for a reason.

We ventured deeper into the headmaster's quarters, reaching a place I had never been before. I watched as Antonius recited runic incantations under his breath. His fingers danced in the air, tracing intricate patterns that shimmered before fading. And then, before my eyes, a secret door appeared. It was as if the wall itself had parted, revealing a concealed entrance that had been invisible to my eyes.

"Follow me," Antonius commanded, waving his hand. The door swung open silently, and we stepped into an unseen world.

A second later, we were engulfed by magic. With another runic marking from Antonius, the room sprung to life. Tomes flew off the shelves, hovering and spinning in the air. Arcane light in the form of an Owl passed through me, its spectral feathers leaving trails of illuminating energy. Swords and staffs, artifacts of the ancient times, floated around us in a mesmerizing dance. The air was electric, buzzing with raw, uncontained magic. It was the most beautiful thing I'd ever seen.

"Kolos," Antonius' voice sounded distant as I remained rooted in place, awestruck by the spectacle. He had continued walking, his figure just a silhouette against the enchanting display of magic.

Shaking off my stupor, I followed Antonius through the sea of floating tomes and weapons. As I reached him, Antonius turned to face me. His eyes, reflecting the myriad of lights, held an intensity I hadn't seen before.

"Kolos," he said, his voice steady. "What I am about to show you, no one else has seen before."

Chapter 7

Antonius' hand reached out and gently grasped an old wooden box that was as beautiful as it was ancient. The box floated in the air, levitating through the magic Antonius had harnessed. His voice broke through the whispers of magic around us, "Open it, Kolos."

With a nod, I extended my hand. The lid of the box creaked open, revealing the unthinkable: a lightning heart, pulsing with life and energy. The sight was horrifying and breathtaking all at once, and I recoiled, a gasp escaping my lips. "You... you killed it? For power?" I accused, my voice trembling with disbelief and anger.

"No, Kolos. No," Antonius responded, his voice filled with a mixture of regret and sorrow. "I was ready to. I had looked for the fox for years, motivated by power and ambition. I was prepared to take its life if necessary. But when I found her, she was already dying."

The word "her" lingered in the air. The fox, the legendary storm fox, was a *she*.

"She had a mortal wound in her chest. A wound that should've killed her months before I found her," Antonius continued, his voice barely above a whisper. "But she held on, bled her spirit and essence slowly for months. And when I was ready to end her life, she looked at me."

Antonius' eyes were far away now, lost in the memory. "There was peace in her eyes. She had endured so much pain, for so long. And then I understood why. She was protecting her children. Four beautiful cubs. She could not let herself die until she found someone who would care for them."

Antonius' gaze met mine. "I dropped my staff that day, Kolos. I promised her I would protect her children. As long as I draw breath, nothing will harm them."

A heavy silence filled the room, the weight of the revelation sinking in. Then Antonius spoke again, "If you wish to see the truth of my words, touch her heart. She will show you."

Chapter 8

With a hesitant touch, I connected with the fox's heart. A jolt of energy surged through me as I was plunged into a torrent of memories and emotions. I could see the world through her eyes, feel her pain, her relief, her hope. I saw her last moments, how she willingly gave her essence to Antonius. Her magic now flowed through him, her legacy living on through her children.

I saw her memories of Antonius, the man who had once sought to claim her power, taking her cubs to safety. I felt her trust in him, the assurance that he would keep his promise. I saw the moment she bestowed her arcane spirit upon him, marking him as worthy of her power.

The trance faded, and I was back in the room, the heart still pulsating in the box. My heart pounded in sync with the rhythm, the raw power of the experience still lingering.

"Are her children... are they alive?" I asked, my voice barely a whisper.

Antonius looked at me, his gaze intimidating.

"They are safe," he said, his voice low but firm. "And if anyone ever tries to harm them, I will kill them. Even you, son."

The threat hung in the air, but I nodded. "I would never hurt them. Not after what I've seen."

I left the headmaster's quarters then, my mind reeling with the memories I had seen, the raw power I had felt. The last echoes of an ancient being, the magic that had flowed through her veins, it was overwhelming.

As I laid in my bed that night, staring up at the ceiling of the dormitory, I couldn't help but think about the power I had witnessed, the potential it held. I was just a student, yet there had to be something I could do to amplify my power. But what?

The question lingered in my mind as I drifted off to sleep, the images of the day dancing in my dreams.

Legend of the Ice Demon

Chapter 9

Barely able to contain my excitement, I rushed to the conservatory's magical library as soon as my eyes fluttered open. I was on a mission, a quest to find more about magic amplification. The library, a repository of arcane knowledge, was my battlefield.

With a heart full of determination, I poured over countless books, tomes, and scrolls, completely engrossed in my search. The world outside the library ceased to exist. I ignored my hunger and thirst, so absorbed was I in my quest.

After a day of relentless pursuit, I finally found what I was looking for. A dusty, ancient tome dedicated to magic amplification and magical creatures. It contained details about the storm fox, the phoenix, and the sea owl.

The storm fox I knew about - its essence was now a part of Antonius. The phoenix, a creature of pure fire and spirit, was a rare sight, emerging once every hundred years or so to pick a worthy champion. The sea owl was believed to have gone extinct a thousand years ago.

Just as I was about to close the tome, a new page caught my attention. It spoke of another creature, unlike the benevolent ones I had read about before. This one was different. It was a creature of unimaginable evil, a being of extreme power - the Ice Demon.

According to the tome, the Ice Demon had claimed countless lives of those who had tried to harness its power. A shiver ran down my spine as I read the tales of its wrath. This was a creature not to be trifled with.

Chapter 10

The library was still, a cathedral of silence broken only by the muted rustle of ancient pages turning and the rhythmic ticking of a distant clock. I stood there, an island amidst the ocean of knowledge, a forbidden tome clutched in my hands. "Mythical Creatures and Magical Amplification," it read. It was a volume unlike any other I had seen, and I felt an inexplicable pull towards it. A pull that defied rules and regulations.

In a flurry of nerves, I secreted it away under my cloak and walked out of the library. Each footstep echoed with a note of guilt, but the thirst for knowledge was too potent, too intoxicating to resist. Back in the safety of my quarters, I unveiled the tome, its old leather cover cool under my fingertips. I began to delve into its secrets.

The Storm Fox, the Phoenix, the Sea Owl - their stories were written down, their powers explained, their essence captured in ink. The Phoenix, a creature of rebirth, only choosing a champion once every hundred years. The Sea Owl, a being of wisdom and water, extinct for a thousand years. As I read, I could almost hear their distant calls, feel the echo of their powers. But the true chilling tale lay further in, a tale of a creature as old as time itself, filled with power and malice – the Ice Demon. It was said to inhabit the barren wastes of the north, in the forgotten continent beyond the dreadful expanse. Every soul who sought the Ice Demon had perished, their stories silenced by the icy grip of death.

I was so absorbed in the tale of one such ill-fated adventurer that I almost missed the knock on the door. Panic surged through me. I hastily hid the tome under my bed and rushed to the door. With a deep breath to steady my racing heart, I pulled it open to reveal Antonius Silverhand, my mentor, his silvery eyes inscrutable.

"Kolos," he began, a strange edge to his normally warm tone. "May I come in?" His request hung in the air, a question that felt more like a verdict waiting to be passed. A chill ran down my spine, and I found myself lost in a moment of indecision. What would he think of me if he knew what I'd done? Could he already suspect?

Swallowing my apprehension, I nodded, opening the door wider to let him in. "Of course, Headmaster," I said, trying to keep my voice steady. "Please, come in." The door closed behind him with a soft click, a sound that felt like the final tick of a countdown. I turned to face him, my heart pounding in my chest. The next few moments would decide everything.

Chapter 11

Antonius had been my mentor for years, but in that moment, as he stepped into my small, cluttered quarters, he seemed less a master and more a father. I watched him take in the room, his eyes moving over the stacks of parchment, the half-finished spells, the small bed pushed against one wall. Then, his gaze landed on me.

"Kolos," he began, his voice softer than I had expected. "I see in you the same fire that once burned within me. A desire to prove yourself, to grasp power and make it your own. I understand it, more than you might believe. But there is something you must remember."

He paused, his silvery eyes holding mine. "The way to power is not through desperation. It is through compassion, determination, and patience. Power gained in haste or in anger is power that burns quickly and dies. But power earned through hard work, through understanding and humility—that is the power that lasts."

His words hung in the air, heavy and full of meaning. I struggled to make sense of them, to reconcile them with the urgency I felt deep in my core. I wanted to object, to argue, to tell him he was wrong. But the look in his eyes stopped me. It was a look of understanding, of having been where I was now.

"I was like you once," he continued, his voice tinged with memories of a past long gone. "Thirsty for arcane energy, for power, for recognition. I wanted to be the greatest mage who ever lived, to surpass all those who came before me. And I was ready to take that power by force. But I was wrong. It was only when I learned to control my desires, to be patient, to wait for the power to be freely given, that I truly became strong."

He paused, studying me. "I'm an old man, Kolos. One day, sooner or later, someone will need to take my place as headmaster. I see in you the potential to be that person. But you must learn patience. You must learn to make wise decisions."

I met his gaze, my heart pounding. "I'm not like you, Antonius," I said, my voice shaking slightly. "I'm not... I'm not the person to be headmaster."

He smiled, a small, sad smile. "Perhaps not now, Kolos. But I see the mage you can become."

As he moved towards the door, I found the courage to ask the question that had been haunting me. "Antonius," I called, and he turned to face me. "What do you know about the Ice Demon?" The words hung in the air, a question left unanswered as the room fell into silence.

Chapter 12

The mention of the Ice Demon had a visible effect on Antonius. His face, normally composed and serene, was etched with worry. He turned to face me, his eyes searching mine. "Where did you hear about this?" he demanded. "What books have you been reading?"

"Just...just this old tome I found at the library," I stammered, my heart pounding. "It's about mythical creatures and..."

"Magical amplification," he finished for me, his voice heavy. He moved closer, his face grave. "Kolos, I warn you now. Stay away from such stories. They are nothing but legends, tales spun by imaginative minds. No one has ever seen the Ice Demon. If it even exists, anyone who has seen it hasn't lived to tell the tale."

"But the Storm Fox was just a legend too, and you found it," I countered, trying to keep my voice steady. "Why can't the Ice Demon be real as well?"

The look Antonius gave me was one I had never seen before. It was a stern, almost fatherly look, filled with a mixture of concern and disappointment. He grabbed my arm, his grip firm. "Listen to me, Kolos. You will stop this at once. I forbid you to continue reading about these things. Nothing good can come from it. Stay away from it. Do you understand?"

I nodded, swallowing hard. "Yes, Antonius," I managed to say, my voice barely above a whisper.

"Very well," he said, releasing my arm. "I will see you at first light for your training session." With that, he turned and left, closing the door quietly behind him.

I sat on my bed, my mind racing. His words echoed in my head, a warning I couldn't ignore. Yet, a part of me still yearned for the power the Ice Demon was said to possess.

As if sensing my turmoil, the Flying Codex I had been gifted earlier fluttered towards me. It opened on its own, a screen popping up with words I hadn't expected to see. "Quest Received: Find the Ice Demon". Below it, two options presented themselves. "Accept quest" or "Ignore quest".

I stared at the screen, my heart pounding. I was at a crossroads, and the decision I made here would undoubtedly shape my future. The room fell silent as I pondered over my next move.

Joel Poe

Chapter 13

The moon hung high in the sky, bathing the Conservatory in a soft, ethereal light. In the quiet of my dorm, the ticking of the clock seemed louder than ever, marking the fleeting seconds. I was packing hurriedly, stuffing my bag with everything I thought I would need - the old tome, my clothes, and some food. The

Flying Codex fluttered about, following me around as if eager to be part of the adventure.

I pulled my cloak over my head, tucking my face into its shadow. One last look around the room, the place that had been my home for years, and then I was ready. My heart was heavy with the thought of leaving, of disobeying Antonius, someone who had given me so much. I could already picture the disappointment in his eyes, but this was something I had to do.

Before I left, I penned a quick note for Antonius. A farewell of sorts, an apology, a promise to return. I left it on my desk, the ink still wet.

My quest had just begun. I had to make it past Professor Silvia Froggenstale, the old witch who was in charge of the Conservatory's defenses. Despite her kind demeanor, she was formidable when provoked. Her eyes missed nothing, her ears caught every sound.

The HUD of my Codex sprung to life. As I scrolled through my inventory, my fingers stopped at a small vial labeled 'Invisibility Potion'. It was a gamble, a risky one at that. The potion would only last for 30 seconds.

Teleportation would have been easier, but the Conservatory was shielded against such magic, a barrier maintained by Antonius himself. Any attempt at teleportation would instantly alert him.

With a deep breath, I uncorked the vial and downed the potion. The world around me shimmered as I turned invisible. The countdown began - 30 seconds.

My heart pounded in my chest as I darted through the deserted hallways. The seconds ticked by quickly, too quickly. The potion was about to wear off.

I burst through the final hallway, the gates of the Conservatory coming into view. And standing there, her figure illuminated by the moonlight, was Professor Silvia Froggenstale.

Chapter 14

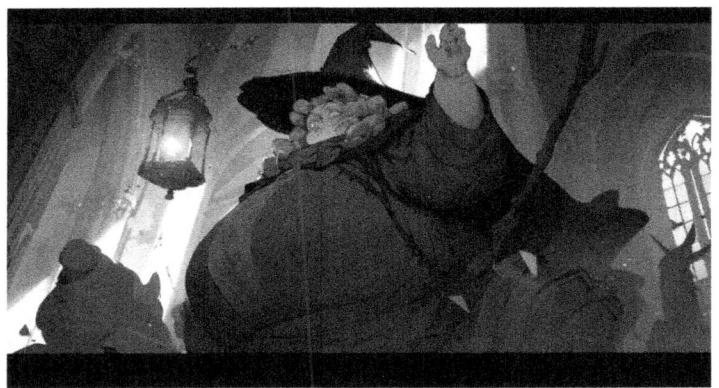

My heart pounded in my chest as the seconds on my invisibility potion ticked away. Only fifteen remained. I had to make a decision, and I had to make it fast. I stared at the enormous figure of Professor Froggenstale, her large body blocking the exit like a giant boulder in the way of my escape.

The Flying Codex whirred to life, opening up before me to reveal the glowing interface of the HUD. Two options were displayed on the screen. The first: attempt to walk past Professor Froggenstale unnoticed. The second: use a snaring incantation to render her unconscious for five minutes.

Neither option was particularly enticing. Trying to slip past her unnoticed seemed almost impossible. With her heightened senses, she would most likely detect me the moment I got too close. She could dispel my invisibility, leaving me exposed instantly.

The second option wasn't much better. Yes, the snaring incantation could incapacitate her for five minutes, but it came with its own risks. Professor Froggenstale had a formidable magic resistance aura, a characteristic of her witch class. If she resisted my spell, I would be caught immediately.

Yet, I had one advantage: I was still invisible. She wouldn't see the spell coming until it was too late. But for it to work, I would have to pour a significant amount of my mana into it.

With only seconds remaining, I made my decision. I chose the second option.

My hands quickly formed the intricate gestures needed for the snaring incantation. I channeled my mana into the spell, feeling it drain from me as I did. I released the spell towards Professor Froggenstale.

The spell hit its mark. She slumped to the ground, unconscious.

I sprinted past her, out of the gates of the Conservatory, and into the cool night beyond. As I did, the Flying Codex whirred to life once more, the HUD displaying a new message: "Side Quest Completed: Escape the Conservatory".

Chapter 15

The blanket of night had settled over the city when I finally extricated myself from the confines of the conservatory. The buildings loomed ominously, their silhouettes stark against the star-speckled sky. My heart pounded in my chest, a percussive accompaniment to the surreal symphony of my escape.

The city was a labyrinth of narrow alleyways and bustling streets, but my feet seemed to know where to take me. Drawn by an inexplicable magnetism, I found myself standing before a cheap motel, its neon sign flickering like an erratic heartbeat. It was far from luxurious, but it promised sanctuary from the biting chill of the night.

Upon entering, I was greeted by the sight of a woman who seemed incongruously attractive for such a place. Her age was hard to pin down, though I guessed she was in her 40s or early 50s. Despite the lines etched into her face, a youthful vitality shone through her eyes.

Feigning nonchalance, I approached the counter and asked if there was a vacant room. She looked me over, her gaze as sharp as a falcon's, and asked, "What's a young mage doing in this part of the city at this hour?"

The question hung in the air between us, but instead of answering directly, I let a playful grin tug at the corners of my mouth. "I could ask you the same," I retorted, "what's such a beautiful lady like yourself doing running a cheap motel like this?"

Her cheeks flushed a rosy hue, and she confessed that she was the owner, having inherited the motel from her grandfather. Our conversation flowed easily, filled with flirty banter and shared laughter. As she handed me the key to my room, I couldn't resist extending an invitation. "You're welcome to join me later if you want to continue our conversation," I said, leaving the invitation hanging in the air like an unfinished melody.

Once in my room, I finally felt the full weight of the day's events. I shed my shoes and shirt, the cool air of the room prickling my skin. Sitting cross-legged on the threadbare carpet, I pulled out the ancient tome about the Ice Demon. The weight of the book in my hands was a solid reminder of the journey I had embarked upon.

As I lost myself in the labyrinthine tales and cryptic illustrations, a knock at the door jolted me back to reality. I opened the door to find the motel owner standing there. Her presence was unexpected, yet not unwelcome.

I flashed her a smile, an unspoken invitation hanging in the air between us. She returned the smile and took a step into the room. With a soft click, I closed the door behind her, sealing us away from the world outside.

Chapter 16

The ambient glow of the motel's neon sign filtered through the gauzy curtains, bathing the room in a spectral light. We were sprawled across the bed, our conversation punctuated by laughter and playful jabs.

Her question broke through our light-hearted exchange. "How old are you, Kolos?"

"I'm 21," I replied nonchalantly, watching as surprise danced in her eyes.

"That was pretty good for a 21-year-old," she said, a mischievous glint in her eye.

Chuckling, I shot back, "Stop pretending. Your screams didn't lie, and your nails left their mark on my back. What are you, a cat?" We both dissolved into laughter, the echoes of our mirth bouncing off the motel room walls.

Once the laughter subsided, her playful demeanor changed slightly, her gaze piercing me with curiosity. "Why are you here, Kolos? Did you run away from the conservatory?"

Her question hit its mark. I sighed, gazing up at the cracked ceiling. "It's a long story, but yes, I ran away. I have something I need to take care of."

A moment of silence passed before curiosity nudged me to ask, "By the way, how old are you? You never told me."

She chuckled lightly, an amused smirk playing on her lips. "A lady doesn't reveal her age."

"But surely you can make an exception for me?" I implored, putting on my most charming smile.

Laughing, she acquiesced, "Alright, alright. I'm 52."

My eyes widened slightly. "Really? How do you stay in such good shape?"

"Well," she said, propping herself up on one elbow to look at me. "I'm a healer. I know a thing or two about taking care of the body."

An appreciative grin spread across my face. "I knew it. I've always had a thing for healers."

"Oh, did you now?" she asked, her voice a blend of amusement and intrigue.

"Mhm," I replied, my grin turning into a playful smirk. "Hey, I have to leave soon. But how about we do it my way now?"

She raised an eyebrow, curiosity piqued. "And what is your way?"

I flipped her upside down with a swift motion, flashing her a wicked grin. "You might have to scream a bit louder this time."

As the room filled with our laughter once more, I savored the fleeting moments of this unexpected rendezvous, the weight of my journey temporarily forgotten.

Chapter 17

Morning dawned, the city awakening in soft pastels as the sun began its ascent into the sky. In our secluded corner of the world, time seemed to stand still. She was still in bed, a vision of matured beauty, her eyes tracing my form as I dressed.

In the dim morning light, my body appeared carved from marble, every line and muscle accentuated. Her gaze was fixed on my exposed back, her eyes following the network of well-defined muscles that had been concealed beneath my mage's robe.

"Are you sure you can't stay a few more days?" she asked, her voice tinged with regret. "It's on the house."

I paused, looking over at her. "Believe me, I would if I could," I confessed, my voice carrying a note of genuine regret. "But by this time, the headmaster probably noticed my absence. He'll have the paragons scouring the city for me. I can't go back there, not until I've found what I'm looking for."

"Pity," she sighed, her gaze not leaving my form. "I really enjoyed 'your way'."

My laughter echoed in the small room, a rare moment of light-heartedness in the face of my looming journey. "I'll make sure to come by another time when I return," I promised, locking my eyes with hers.

The air crackled with unspoken promise as I approached the bed. Bending over, I claimed her lips with an aggressive kiss that sent sparks cascading down my spine. After a few breathless moments, I pulled away slightly, a playful grin adorning my face. "You know what? How about a parting gift?"

Her eyes sparkled with intrigue as she leaned back on the pillows. "What do you have in mind?"

A devilish smile played on my lips as I began to unbutton my pants. Her laughter filled the room, mingling with the early morning sunlight filtering through the window. "Yes," she said, a cheeky grin on her face, "we can do that."

Chapter 18

The morning sunlight spilled into the motel room, casting long shadows as I prepared to take my leave. The bed was a rumpled memory of our night together, a silent testimony of the passion we'd shared.

As I was about to cross the threshold, Atia appeared, holding out two small vials. The liquid inside them glowed with a gentle luminescence, the mark of well-brewed healing potions.

"You might have need of these on your journey," she said, her voice softer than I'd heard it before.

I gratefully accepted the potions, tucking them into my bag. "Thank you, Atia," I said. The name felt foreign on my tongue, yet oddly fitting. "You kept me so busy I didn't even have the chance to ask your name till just this morning."

She chuckled lightly at that, her eyes dancing with a shared mischief.

"By the way, Atia," I began, my voice dipping into a playful tone. "You never told me you were also a vampire."

Her laughter filled the room, a pleasant melody that eased the burden of my impending departure. "Why would you say that?" she asked, raising an amused eyebrow at my jest.

"Well, I better not say what I'm thinking," I retorted with a teasing grin.

We both broke into laughter, the sound echoing in the small motel room. Our shared mirth felt like a balm, a buffer against the harsh reality of our imminent separation.

With a final glance around the room, I knew it was time to leave. "Alright, I better go now," I said, the words a harsh reminder of the duty I had to fulfill.

As I turned to leave, I grabbed Atia by her neck, pulling her in for one last kiss. It was a promise, a farewell, and a thank you all wrapped into one. I could feel her smile against my lips as I finally pulled away, the door closing softly behind me.

Chapter 19

Stepping out of the motel's shadow, I took one last glance at the neon sign before venturing into the sprawling labyrinth of the city. I could feel the morning sun warm against my skin, a stark contrast to the chilly air that had accompanied the night's events. As I moved further into the city, towards the outskirts, my heart pounded in my chest - each beat a pulsating reminder of my looming journey.

However, my departure from the city was interrupted by a formidable trio that seemed to materialize out of thin air. They were the paragons, high-level mages dispatched by the headmaster, Antonius. Dressed in robes that denoted their rank and power, they stood imposingly in front of me, blocking my path.

"Kolos," their leader spoke, his voice resonating with an authoritative timbre, "you need to come back to the conservatory."

I met his gaze, my resolve unyielding. "I have no intention of going back," I replied, my tone equally resolute.

"You can come back with us peacefully," he continued, "or by force."

A smirk tugged at the corners of my mouth as I retorted, "I prefer option three."

One of the paragons, a burly man with a stern face, looked perplexed. "What is option three?" he asked.

As the words left his mouth, I swiftly recited an incantation under my breath. A stunning spell hit him before he could react, rendering him unconscious. Without a second thought, I turned on my heel and ran, the clatter of my boots against the cobblestone streets echoing through the city's air.

The remaining paragons were quick to recover, giving chase as I weaved through the maze of the city. I dashed through narrow alleyways and crowded markets. Steam engines hissed and gears clicked as I darted around horse-drawn carriages, always one step ahead of the chasing paragons.

After several heart-stopping moments, I managed to shake them off my trail, the sounds of their pursuit fading into the morning bustle of the city.

Far enough from the conservatory, I could finally perform a teleportation spell. The flying codex sprung open, projecting a holographic screen.

"Teleport to Shadowing Woods," it proposed.

I grimaced at the suggestion. The Shadowing Woods were notorious for their dangerous inhabitants. I paused, weighing the risk. But then, the thought struck me: Antonius and his paragons would never think of searching for me in such a perilous location. It was the perfect hideout.

With a sigh of resignation, I agreed to the codex's quest. I uttered the complex incantation, weaving the tapestry of my escape. As the world around me began to dissolve, I prepared myself to face the unknown dangers that awaited me in the Shadowing Woods.

Chapter 20

As the teleportation spell released me, I found myself standing amidst the dreadful expanse of the Shadowing Woods. Even in daylight, the forest was shrouded in an eerie twilight, its towering trees blocking out the sun's rays. The atmosphere was stifling, a claustrophobic collage of shadow and decay.

Gritting my teeth, I began to navigate through the undergrowth, keeping an eye out for a safe place to establish a makeshift camp. The forest remained eerily silent, save for the rustling of leaves and the occasional snap of twigs beneath my boots.

Suddenly, an unsettling rustle echoed through the silence. I froze, turning towards the sound to find a giant black spider emerging from the foliage. Its massive, grotesque form sent a shiver down my spine. It was a shadow monster, the likes of which inhabited the darkest corners of this forest. Its myriad eyes focused on me, and I knew I was its next meal.

I quickly shifted to battle stance, gathering my mana. My HP was full, at 200, but I had to use my resources wisely. The spider lunged, and the battle began.

I cast 'Arcane Blast,' a projectile of pure arcane energy that ripped through the air towards the spider. It hit, deducting 20 points from the spider's HP. The spider retaliated with a volley of shadow venom, depleting my HP by 30 points. We exchanged spells, a dangerous dance in the shadowy theatre of the forest.

In a swift move, the spider cast 'Shadow Web.' A dark, viscous web spun out towards me. Too late to dodge, I found myself ensnared, my movements restricted. My mana was low, and I was caught like prey in the spider's trap. As the spider advanced for the kill, my vision began to blur.

Suddenly, an ethereal howl filled the air. A burst of radiant light flooded the area, revealing an old orc shaman, his arms raised as he summoned the spirits of the earth and forest. Phantom wolves materialized from thin air, their forms glowing with a spectral light. They charged at the spider, their spectral teeth biting into its shadowy flesh, deducting massive chunks from its HP.

The orc didn't stop there. With a guttural chant, he called forth bolts of lightning from the heavens, zapping the spider. The spider shrieked and retreated, disappearing into the forest's shadowy depths.

I let out a breath I didn't realize I'd been holding. But the relief was short-lived. My vision began to wane, the edges growing dark. The last thing I saw was the orc shaman approach, kneeling beside me as my consciousness slipped away.

Chapter 21

I awoke to the warm glow of a fire and the surprisingly comforting surroundings of a humble dwelling carved out from the forest itself. The scent of the earth and the crackle of the flames provided a soothing contrast to the oppressive gloom of the Shadowing Woods. I was in the lair of the orc shaman.

"Thank you for saving me," I said, my voice echoing my gratitude. "It's good to know there are uncorrupted orcs still out there."

The old shaman simply nodded, bringing forth a bowl of fragrant soup. "Eat, it will make you strong," he said, his deep voice gentle.

Accepting the bowl, I nodded in thanks and began to eat. The savory broth was warming, filling me with a sense of renewed strength.

After a few moments, the orc shaman asked, "What is a young mage doing in the forbidden Shadowing Woods? Nobody comes here."

His question hung in the air, punctuated by the crackling of the fire. I sighed, deciding to be honest. "I ran away from the conservatory. I seek the Ice Demon."

His eyes widened slightly. "Only fools seek the Ice Demon," he muttered, more to himself than to me. But he provided cryptic clues to the Ice Demon's whereabouts and gave me a strange artifact, pulsing with power. He warned me that I had to leave at first light. The shadow creatures, attracted by my arcane mana, would overrun his abode.

Understanding his concern, I asked a question of my own, "Why don't they sense your mana, shaman?"

"I use spirit, not mana," he responded.

Confused, I jokingly asked if they weren't the same thing. But he explained, "Similar, but not remotely the same. Mana is energy from one's own soul. Spirit is energy from the ancestors that flows through me. I am but a conduit."

I contemplated this, the idea intriguing. But my fatigue was creeping back, pulling me towards sleep. As I set down the empty soup bowl, I thanked the shaman for his hospitality. Leaning back, I closed my eyes, knowing that when I awoke, my journey would take another step forward.

Chapter 22

Dawn had just started to break, stretching pale fingers across the skyline, when I stirred from my slumber. My eyes fluttered open to the sight of the elderly orc shaman, his hands busy crafting a magical staff.

"That's a fine looking staff," I commented, pushing myself into a sitting position. "What's it for?"

The orc didn't look up from his task. "You're powerful, young mage, but your arcane power lacks discipline," he said, his voice deep and gravelly.

"This staff will help you channel your magic more efficiently. It's for you."

Accepting the staff from the orc, I marveled at the craftsmanship. The wood felt solid in my grasp, and as I held it, I could feel the pulsating flow of arcane magic. I murmured my gratitude to the old shaman.

"It's time you leave now," he declared, his gaze now locked on mine. "Your presence has stirred the forest, setting in motion events darker than I'd sensed before. The spirits are angry."

The thought sent a chill down my spine. "Which way to the nearest city?" I asked, my thoughts flitting to potential sanctuaries.

"The nearest city is Daileem," he replied, a note of sorrow in his voice. "But it's fallen entirely under Malazar's influence. Overrun by undead and undertakers, no one gets in or out."

My heart clenched at the mention of Daileem. I remembered that city all too well. It was where I'd grown up as a slave, where I'd made my first kill by impaling the Baron's throat with ice shards formed from his own saliva. The memories flooded back, stoking the embers of my fury.

"Be careful, young mage," the shaman warned, interrupting my turbulent thoughts. "Your rage will only feed the hateful spirits that inhabit this forest. You must travel north and do not use teleportation spells until you step foot outside the boundaries of the Shadowing Woods."

Nodding my understanding, I thanked the orc shaman one last time and left his humble abode. I ventured back into the cold, dreary forest, the weight of his warning heavy on my mind. Why had he cautioned against using teleportation spells in the forest? What lurked in the shadows of the trees? As I ventured into the heart of the forest, I couldn't help but feel an uncanny sense of unease.

Chapter 23

The Shadowing Woods were not only a landscape of gnarled trees and overgrown vegetation. They were also a landscape of dread, of ancient horrors and enigmatic mysteries. One such mystery was an abandoned temple I came across as I delved deeper into the woods.

The ancient structure was nestled amongst the trees, half-concealed by the twisted undergrowth. Its stone façade bore runes of an ancient dialect, whispering stories of forgotten epochs. It pulsed with an eerie energy, a dark resonance that seemed to hum in the very air. Despite the temptation to explore, the aura of evil was palpable and I quickened my pace, determined to put distance between myself and the forsaken place.

But the woods weren't finished with me yet. As I trudged onward, I found myself intercepted by three grotesque creatures. Their shrill caw echoed through the quiet woods, the eerie sound a jarring contrast to the silence. With rotting flesh hanging off their skeletal bodies and beaks half broken, half necrotized, they were an abomination to the eye – undead Harpies.

The sight of these undead in the woods was unexpected. Weren't all undead under Malazar's dominion? Were these creatures too repulsive even for him? Questions spun in my mind, but one fact was certain. They were level 57, 53, and 35 respectively – formidable foes, especially for someone unable to use teleportation within the confines of these woods.

A grim determination settled within me. I was outmatched, but running wasn't an option. I couldn't outrun Harpies, and the old orc's warning against teleportation in the woods echoed in my mind. So, it seemed my path was clear. These abominations had to be dealt with, no matter how repugnant the task. With a firm grip on my staff and a stern gaze set on the impending foes, I steeled myself for the upcoming battle.

Chapter 24

I steeled myself for the impending fight, gripping the new staff in my hand. Its familiar, comforting weight felt good. My gaze took in the three harpies. 57, 53, 35 – those numbers swirled in my mind. Formidable foes, especially for a level 21 Arcane Mage like myself. But I had no other choice.

Summoning up my mana, I watched as my mana bar filled to the brim – 100/100. The brilliant blue energy rippled around me, crackling in the charged air. My health was also at its full capacity. With a deep breath, I released my first spell, "Arcane Bolts!" The incantation, reverberating in the air around me, sent streaks of arcane energy spiraling towards the undead Harpies.

My eyes watched as the bolts struck their targets. A triumphant smile crept onto my face as two of the harpies screeched, their HP dropping. The level 57 harpy went down to 50/70 HP, while the level 53 harpy dropped to 40/60 HP. But the level 35 harpy dodged, her HP remaining untouched at 30/30.

I felt a thrill of victory, but it was short-lived. With horrifying speed, the level 57 Harpy lunged at me, her talons sharp and deadly. I barely managed to raise a defensive spell, "Arcane Shield!", but it wasn't enough. I grunted in pain as her talons slashed through my arcane shield.

Ignoring the sting of pain, I retaliated with another "Arcane Bolts!" This time all three bolts found their marks. The level 57 and 53 harpies were down to 25/70 and 15/60 HP respectively, while the level 35 harpy dropped to 20/30. But my mana was also depleting. I was now down to 70/100.

The Harpies screeched again, an ear-piercing sound that echoed off the gnarled trees. In a coordinated attack, they lunged. Despite my efforts to dodge and weave, their talons caught me again and again. My HP dropped steadily.

Pushing through the pain, I knew I needed a game-changer. Focusing all my remaining mana, I conjured a more potent spell. "Arcane Explosion!" I bellowed. A shockwave of arcane energy erupted from me. The forest shuddered, the ground beneath us quaking as my spell ripped through the surroundings.

The Harpies were thrown backward, their screeches of surprise mingling with the thunderous boom of my spell. The level 57 and 53 harpies collapsed, their HP hitting zero. Their bodies disintegrated into wisps of shadow that were swallowed by the dark forest.

But the level 35 harpy was resilient. Even with her HP down to a mere 5/30, she rose again, screeching in fury. I was down to a critical HP, and completely out of mana. My heart pounded in my chest. I knew I had one last move.

Summoning the last vestiges of my strength, I swung my staff. It connected with a sickening crunch. The harpy squawked in surprise and pain as her HP dropped to zero. She disintegrated just like her companions, leaving me alone in the eerie silence of the forest.

A surge of power rushed through me, as the world seemed to hold its breath. The characteristic ding of leveling up echoed in the quiet forest. A message from the universe, proclaiming my victory against insurmountable odds. Level 22, the codex read, and I felt a surge of satisfaction, mixed with the bone-deep weariness of battle.

With the last of the Harpies gone, I sank to my knees, panting heavily. My health bar was dangerously low, and my mana was completely depleted. But despite the pain, I felt a sense of triumph. I had survived the Shadowing Woods, survived the Harpies. For now, at least, I was safe. As I sat there, drawing ragged breaths, I knew one thing for certain. I had a long, perilous journey ahead of me. But I was ready.

Chapter 25

The echoes of battle still rang in my ears as I moved away from the brutal scene of my clash with the harpies. Each step was a reminder of the grueling fight; my body felt like lead, and every muscle protested. Yet, the victorious thrill that coursed through my veins overshadowed any discomfort. I could feel my power growing, my connection to the arcane strengthening. But my health and mana bars were severely depleted, and I needed to rest.

I came upon the remnants of a city swallowed by time and nature. Crumbling stone structures, etched with ancient symbols and pictographs, told of a civilization lost to history: the centaurs. I traced the faded carvings with my fingers, taking in the melancholy beauty of these forgotten souls. They had once been a proud and powerful race, hunted down and slaughtered for being different, for daring to exist outside the norms set by narrow-minded human rulers.

Now, only their restless spirits lingered. The air around me felt thick with sorrow, the agony of an entire species echoed in the silent whispers of the wind. I had felt the resonance of the forest since stepping into it, but now, among the remnants of the centaur civilization, it was a palpable presence.

Could their lingering pain be the cause of the shadowing woods' corruption? Was the forest's darkness merely a reflection of the anguish that inhabited it? As I moved deeper into the city, the spirits seemed to sense my thoughts, my sympathy for their fate. They didn't fight me; instead, they seemed to guide me, their spectral forms flickering on the edges of my vision.

Finding a relatively intact structure, I decided to set up camp for the night. As the fire crackled to life, casting dancing shadows on the worn stone walls around me, I couldn't help but think about the echoes of laughter and chatter that once filled these streets. Now, it was only a ghost city, a chilling monument of past cruelty.

I reached into my bag, retrieving one of the healing potions Atia had given me. The warmth that spread through my veins was a soothing balm against the harsh coldness of the woods, and my health bar began to slowly replenish. A sigh escaped my lips as the pain started to recede, my body absorbing the restorative energy from the potion.

The wind seemed to hum a mournful lullaby as I curled up near the fire, wrapping myself in my cloak. Sleep was always elusive after a battle, the adrenaline rush slowly fading away leaving a lingering buzz in my mind.

But exhaustion won eventually. As I drifted into the world of dreams, I spared one last thought for the lost centaurs and the spectral presences that had guided me through their city.

Sleep came as a peaceful darkness, wrapping me in a gentle oblivion, away from the chilling dread of the forest. The ghosts of the centaurs watched over my rest, their sorrowful whispers fading into the rustling leaves. A new day awaited, and with it, the next leg of my journey.

Chapter 26

I woke to the smell of something charred and putrid, an alarming scent that quickly yanked me from my dreams. Blinking my eyes open, I was met with an unsettling sight. A hulking wyvern, its scales an ominous shade of midnight, stood among the remnants of my fire, its massive wings spreading wide and casting a foreboding shadow over the serene ruins of the ancient city. It was a high level creature - an adversary far beyond my current capabilities.

Above its head, the wyvern's health bar was almost full, a sobering contrast to my own. My health was meager, having not yet recovered from the previous day's fight, and my mana was barely half full. The fight ahead would not be an easy one.

I gripped my new staff, its unfamiliar weight grounding me. I began with defensive measures, calling upon an Arcane Shield. It formed around me in a shimmering sphere, a protective barrier between me and the beast, draining my already limited mana further.

Next, I summoned my Ice Shard Barrage spell. The staff pulsed with my energy, cold and intense, before launching a barrage of icy shards towards the wyvern. They struck its scales, causing it to flinch back. Its health bar wavered slightly, a minor but encouraging decrease.

Reacting to the attack, the wyvern took to the skies. Its wings created a strong gust that nearly knocked me off balance. From above, it dive-bombed towards me, opening its mouth to reveal a deadly glow. A torrent of flames spilled out, barreling towards me. The fire clashed with my Arcane Shield, causing it to flicker under the heat, but it held strong, saving me from the fiery onslaught.

In the sky, the wyvern held an advantage. I had to ground it.

Rummaging through my memories, I recalled a binding spell. It was a gamble, I had never cast this spell before, and it would take a large portion of my remaining mana.

With no other choice, I channeled my energy into the staff, whispering the incantation, "Terra Ligare." The magic coursed from the staff, latching onto the wyvern. The creature let out an ear-piercing shriek as it was forced back to the ground. The beast thrashed and roared, but the spell held, keeping it grounded.

The wyvern's momentary immobility was my chance. I was running low on mana, but I had to press on. I channeled my energy into my staff, preparing for my next attack. The thought of the restless centaur spirits, whose home this wyvern invaded, spurred me on.

I focused on the cold that was building up within my staff. When it felt ready to burst, I unleashed another spell, a Charged Ice Shard. The icy projectile flew from the staff, headed straight towards the grounded wyvern...

Chapter 27

A moment seemed to hang in the balance. The wyvern, caught in my spell, writhed against the restraints of the Terra Ligare, its scaly eyes shining with a blend of fury and fear. It struggled, letting out a guttural roar, but it was firmly bound to the earth. All of my being was focused on the staff, on the channeling of power, on the incantation of the Ice Shard spell. As I drew on my dwindling mana reserves, the energy within my staff pulsed and throbbed, icy and biting.

This was it.

With one final, roaring surge of power, I released the spell. A colossal ice shard, larger than any I had ever created, surged from the staff, racing towards the wyvern with a deadly purpose. It struck true, piercing the beast's scaly hide, its monstrous momentum driving it deep into the writhing creature.

A guttural, pained roar filled the air, followed by a silence that was almost deafening. The beast's struggles ceased, replaced by spasmodic twitches as it grappled with the ice shard impaled in its gut. The shard exploded in a burst of icy splinters, sending a shockwave of gore and scale into the surrounding area. The creature's eyes grew dull and vacant, and then, the colossal wyvern fell, causing the earth beneath me to quake.

I stood panting, my staff heavy in my hands, covered in the wyvern's blood and grime, my chest heaving with every breath. The wyvern's health bar had plummeted to zero, and it was no more than a lifeless carcass now.

A surge of energy coursed through me, like a jolt of lightning, and I knew I had leveled up. The rush was intoxicating, my heart pounding in my chest as I realized that I had not just advanced one level, but two! The wyvern's high-level demise had resulted in a double EXP boost, catapulting me straight to Level 24. Despite the exhaustion, a triumphant grin tugged at my lips. The satisfaction of defeating such a formidable opponent was not a feeling I would soon forget.

Legend of the Ice Demon

As the rush of battle subsided, and the reality of my victory set in, I turned to face the ghostly presence of the centaur spirits. They seemed calmer now, their spectral forms less agitated. They led me through the maze-like ruins of their city, guiding me with an invisible hand. Their city, once a thriving civilization, now a testament to the past, felt like a labyrinth of ruins and secrets.

Finally, they led me to a hidden exit, a path that delved deeper into the shadowing woods, away from their abandoned city. I turned to the spectral figures, feeling an inexplicable bond with these lost souls.

"May you find peace," I uttered, a silent prayer echoing in the quiet ruins. Their response was silent but warm, a subtle glow that faded slowly into the background.

Venturing back into the shadowing woods, the damp chill of the forest closed in around me. But there was a sense of renewed determination in my steps. The encounter with the wyvern, the guidance from the centaur spirits, the leveling up - all of it solidified my resolve.

With the abandoned city at my back, the ruins slowly disappearing behind the tall trees, I ventured deeper into the shadowing woods. The path ahead was fraught with dangers unknown, but for now, I was ready. The journey continued, the road ahead still long and treacherous. But I was Kolos, a mage with a purpose, and I would not be deterred.

Chapter 28

With the wyvern slain and the ancient city of the centaurs behind me, I continued my journey through the shadowing woods, the darkness of the forest slowly giving way to a new challenge: mountains. Fog-shrouded and daunting, they stood before me, their peaks disappearing into the low hanging clouds, veiling them in an aura of mystique.

My heart pounded in my chest as I looked up, a sense of trepidation creeping over me. I had fought and defeated ground and sky monsters, but the idea of climbing these towering giants was intimidating in a whole new way. However, I had no choice. The path forward was clear, and it led straight up into those cloudy peaks.

I started my climb, one careful step at a time, my staff in one hand providing support and my other free to cast spells as needed. The path was treacherous, full of loose rocks and slippery moss, making every footfall a calculated risk. The chilly mountain air bit at my skin, yet it was invigorating, a stark contrast to the dank and oppressive atmosphere of the shadowing woods.

As I ascended, the fog thickened around me, reducing visibility to mere feet. Every rustle of the wind and every shifting of the fog sent me on high alert. In the limited visibility, shadows seemed to shift and dance, turning the harmless into potential threats.

A shrill screech echoed through the fog, making me jump. Emerging from the dense curtain of fog was a monstrous bird, its wingspan vast and ominous. Its health bar appeared as it neared, reading a formidable Level 30.

Without wasting a moment, I channeled my energy into my staff, ready to cast an Ice Shard spell. The creature dove towards me, its talons extended in a predatory stance. As it came closer, I released the spell, sending a flurry of sharp ice shards its way. They hit their mark, causing the monster to screech in pain. However, the damage was less than I had hoped, barely making a dent in its health bar.

The bird retaliated with a gust of wind from its wings, the force of the wind was so strong it nearly knocked me off my feet. I braced myself, realizing that this creature was using wind-based magic, a category of magic I had not yet mastered.

The realization dawned on me. This was not just a fight; this was an opportunity. If I could understand and capture the essence of this wind magic, it would be a valuable addition to my arsenal.

Channeling my focus, I let the creature's magic wash over me, trying to understand its rhythm, its essence. It was wild, unpredictable, yet there was a pattern, a sequence that I could grasp. Slowly, I started to mimic the flow of the magic, replicating its energy within me. The sensation was exhilarating, a new form of magic coursing through me.

Gritting my teeth, I drew upon this newfound power, casting my very first wind-based spell. A gust of wind, similar to the bird's, erupted from my staff. The gust collided with the bird, its impact visible in the creature's surprised expression and the sudden dip in its health bar.

With a newfound sense of determination, I continued my assault. I interspersed my arcane spells with the new wind magic, constantly changing my tactics to keep the monster off balance. It was a grueling battle, a fight that pushed me to my limits. But the final ice shard pierced the bird, dropping its health bar to zero.

With a final screech, it plummeted to the mountainside, its lifeless body disappearing into the fog. I leaned against my staff, panting and weary. But my mana bar was replenishing steadily, and the level-up notification popped up. Level 25.

Legend of the Ice Demon

The taste of victory was sweet, sweeter still was the new spell category unlocked: Wind Magic.

Chapter 29

The mountain path gave way to a thick forest that seemed to absorb all light, plunging everything into a void of inky blackness. A forest unlike the shadowing woods I had just left, a forest that was steeped not in mere darkness but in pure, unadulterated fear. This was a realm of shadows, a place where your deepest fears came alive, testing the strength of your mind and heart.

My heart thudded in my chest as I ventured deeper into the forest. I couldn't see my hand in front of my face, let alone any paths or potential dangers that lurked within this black abyss. My mana bar glowed faintly in the corner of my vision, a reminder that my arcane magic was still within reach.

But what use was magic if you couldn't see your enemy?

As if to answer my silent question, the darkness around me began to stir. Wisps of shadows coalesced, forming shapes in the darkness. Not just any shapes, but forms that dug deep into the crevices of my subconscious, pulling forth my deepest fears.

I stood rooted in place as the first form took shape. A monstrous figure, armed with a whip, his cruel eyes gleaming with sadistic delight. The Baron of Daileem, the man who had turned my childhood into a living hell.

My breath hitched in my throat as he
lunged at me, whip cracking in the air.
On instinct, I raised my staff, prepared
to blast him with an Ice Shard spell.
But my staff passed right through
him, the ice shards dispersing in the
air. He was an illusion, born of my
fears.

No magic seemed to affect him, and
my mana bar remained untouched.
This was not a battle of physical
strength or magical prowess, this was
a battle of will.

Remembering the advice of the hermit
orc shaman, I focused on my inner
strength, on the courage that had
gotten me this far. I had overcome this
fear once before. I could do it again.

With a deep breath, I reached out, letting my hand pass through the illusion. It wavered, then dispersed, leaving nothing but empty air in its place. A sense of relief washed over me, followed by the realization that I had just tapped into a new type of magic - Illusion Magic.

My victory was short-lived as new forms began to emerge from the darkness, each one more terrifying than the last. Friends turned foes, undead hordes, Malazar himself. Each illusion challenged me, pushed me to confront my fears. With each victory, my understanding of Illusion magic deepened.

As hours turned into days, I found myself growing stronger, my will honed with each confrontation. But the darkness offered no respite.

It was then I sensed it - another form of energy coursing through the shadows. Not arcane, not wind, not even illusions. This was different, darker. Shadow Magic.

Much like the wind magic I had learned on the mountain, this magic was wild, uncontrolled, unpredictable. But it was powerful. As I moved deeper into the forest, it began to weave its way into my spells, adding another layer of complexity.

Channeling this shadow magic, I cloaked myself in darkness, becoming one with the shadows. My illusions became more powerful, more convincing. My Ice Shard spell now carried a shadowy aura, its piercing

Legend of the Ice Demon

cold now accompanied by a paralyzing shadow affliction.

As the last remnants of fear were vanquished, my level up notification appeared, blinking brightly in the darkness. Level 26. My journey through the realm of shadows had come to an end. I had faced my fears, learned new abilities, and emerged stronger.

Leaving the shrouded darkness behind, I ventured back into the world of light, ready for the next leg of my journey. The trials were far from over, but I was evolving, becoming stronger with each challenge. I was one step closer to my goal, one step closer to the Ice Demon.

Chapter 30

Finally, I saw it, the threshold where the gnarled roots and spiky thorns of the shadowing woods ceased their hold on the earth. A feeling of victory swept over me as I took the last steps, emerging from the darkness that had been my home and battlefield for the last several days.

I paused, turning back to gaze upon the thick canopy one last time. Shadows danced among the twisted branches, memories of monstrous illusions and blood-curdling fights flickering within their depths. The air still hummed with unseen dangers, the growls of unknown creatures echoing from within. But I was no longer the same novice mage who had stepped into this fearsome realm. I had faced my deepest fears, learned powerful magic, and emerged a victor.

Gratitude swelled in my heart as I silently thanked the old hermit orc shaman, the wandering centaur spirits, and even the fearsome wyvern. Each had played a part in shaping my journey, each had made me stronger.

As I turned my back to the woods, a sense of relief washed over me. I was finally free of its dark grasp. It was time to use the magic I'd been forbidden to use within its depths – the Teleportation spell.

Drawing on my reserves of mana, I focused on my desired destination. An icy fishing town nestled at the foot of a towering mountain, a gateway to the vastness of the dreadful expanse and the frozen continent beyond. I visualized it clearly in my mind, the chill of its air, the crunch of snow beneath my boots, the taste of salt carried on the wind.

With a final flourish of my staff, the arcane symbols of the Teleportation spell took shape around me. My surroundings blurred, then reformed into a new landscape.

Suddenly, the dark, oppressive shadows of the forest were replaced with the stark beauty of a frosted world. A biting cold wind whipped through my cloak as I appeared in the center of a small, icy fishing town. Wooden huts, covered in layers of snow, dotted the landscape, and the smell of fish and sea assaulted my senses.

Fisherfolk turned to stare at me, their eyes wide with surprise. A mage was a rare sight in these parts, a teleporting mage even rarer. I nodded in acknowledgment, then turned my attention to the immediate task at hand.

Warmth, food, and rest.

I made my way towards the local inn, where a welcoming fire roared in the hearth, the smell of hearty stew wafting through the air. Tomorrow, I would need to convince a brave sailor to ferry me across the dreadful expanse. But tonight, I would rest.

And so, with a warm bowl of stew
and the prospect of a soft bed, I
concluded another day on my quest to
find the Ice Demon.

Chapter 31

Awakening from a deep slumber in the rustic bed of the inn, I stretched my arms wide, already feeling the strain of my quest easing slightly. Despite the chill in the air and the frost-covered windows, I felt rested and refreshed.

As I made my way downstairs, the aroma of frying fish and the murmur of early-morning conversation greeted me. Shaking off the remnants of sleep, I tucked into a hearty breakfast, mentally preparing myself for the day's challenge.

Finding a sailor brave or desperate enough to venture into the dreadful expanse was not going to be an easy task. The sea was as mysterious as it was fearsome, and rumors of gigantic sea serpents and deadly whirlpools circulated like wildfire among the townsfolk. But I was undeterred. The Ice Demon awaited, and I was not about to let the fear of the unknown keep me from my quest.

As I ventured out into the bustling port, I was met with a sight of chaos and commerce. Fishermen hauling in their catches, sailors busily mending their nets, the dockside was alive with activity.

I approached sailor after sailor, my plea echoed time and time again – "I need passage across the dreadful expanse". And each time, I was met with the same response. Shaking heads, grimaced faces, and cautionary tales of men who had dared and never returned.

Yet, amid the rejection and the chilling tales, my resolve did not waver. There had to be someone who was willing, someone who could see past the fear.

As the day wore on, my eyes fell upon a young fisherman. A tattered straw hat sat atop his blonde hair, and his boat, worn and weather-beaten, was a stark contrast to the well-kept vessels surrounding it.

His sunburnt face showed signs of hardship, yet his eyes shone with a spirit unbowed. Maybe this was the one.

Approaching him, I once again laid out my request, "I need passage across the dreadful expanse, and I'm willing to pay any price."

His eyes widened at the mention of the expanse, yet he didn't outright refuse. Instead, he regarded me with a long, thoughtful stare before finally breaking the silence, "Are you a mage?" he asked.

I nodded, confirming his query, and his face broke into a crooked grin, "Follow me."

Without any further word, he turned and began walking away, leading the way. Hesitating for only a moment, I fell into step behind him, intrigued and hopeful. Where was he leading me?

Chapter 32

The young fisherman guided me through the icy, narrow streets of the town, the frosty wind biting at our cheeks. We came to a halt in front of an old, ice-encrusted house, the warm glow of firelight flickering through the windows in sharp contrast with the chill outside.

Without a word, the fisherman pushed open the door, revealing a scene that tugged at my heartstrings. An old woman lay shivering on a makeshift bed, her once vibrant eyes now clouded with pain. A pungent aroma of burnt herbs filled the room – a crude attempt at warding off the evil eye, perhaps.

"Mother," he gestured towards the bedridden woman, "is under a curse."

I nodded, understanding why he was ready to risk the journey through the dreadful expanse. His desperation was not rooted in greed or thrill, but in the love for his ailing mother.

I approached the bed, extending a hand to feel the energy that radiated from the woman. The aura that emanated from her was dark, seething, a clear sign of a potent curse. My heart sank. I was no expert in curses, and the one before me was undeniably strong.

"I am no curse-breaker," I admitted, "but I will try my best. However, we'll need a healer."

"Therese," the young fisherman exclaimed, "She's an old healer. Lives on the other side of the town."

"Fetch her. I'll start my preparations," I instructed, hoping the old healer would know a trick or two that could aid us.

Legend of the Ice Demon

As he rushed out of the door, I turned my attention back to the sick woman, now in a state of half-conscious delirium. The faint whisper of incantations under her breath sent shivers down my spine.

Summoning my flying codex, I called upon the wisdom of Antonius. As the words materialized in the air, I scanned the text, attempting to match the symptoms of the cursed woman with the descriptions in the codex.

"Strong binding curse," I muttered under my breath, reading Antonius' words on the subject. "Leads to a gradual weakening of the soul."

The symptoms fit. The woman's life force was slowly being sapped away, her vitality replaced with an icy chill.

Minutes turned into hours as I absorbed the information, trying to make sense of the detailed procedures and incantations that Antonius had outlined. Though he was clear and concise, the gravity of the task was not lost on me. This was going to be no small feat.

The sound of the door creaking open pulled me from my thoughts. The young fisherman had returned, followed by a petite old woman with wispy white hair and sparkling eyes that belied her age. A healer's bag hung over her shoulder, the aroma of herbs wafting through the room.

Legend of the Ice Demon

With her arrival, it was time to take on the challenge that lay ahead.
Preparing to wrestle with the curse, I took a deep breath. We had to lift the curse, not just for the sake of the poor woman, but for the young fisherman who was willing to take me across the dreaded expanse.

Chapter 33

With the first light of dawn creeping into the icy house, I studied the markings on the healer's face, intricate tattoos, shimmering subtly. A realization struck me like a lightning bolt, causing my eyes to widen. "Are you a Srynn?" I asked, the surprise evident in my voice.

Legend of the Ice Demon

The old woman merely responded with a nod. I could hardly believe it. I was under the impression that Malazar had exterminated the Srynn, a gentle and noble race known for their unparalleled healing abilities.

"I thought Malazar had decimated the last of your kind," I confessed, feeling a pang of sadness for the history that had befallen her people.

"There are still a few of us," she replied in her soft, raspy voice, "Hiding in places where the eyes of Malazar's lackeys don't reach."

Her words brought me both relief and sadness. Relief for the survival of such a remarkable race and sadness for the terrifying reality they had to endure.

"Well, lucky for us. Your people were renowned for their healing skills. Let's get to work."

With the young fisherman's anxious gaze upon us, we began the arduous task of extracting the curse. It was a delicate process, like trying to remove a barbed arrow without causing further injury.

As I started the incantations, the eerie glow of my spell casting a surreal luminescence across the room, the curse within the woman began to roil. It squirmed and twisted, trying to dig deeper, to hold on tighter. The strength of it was formidable, but not insurmountable.

Beside me, the Srynn began her work. A gentle glow radiated from her hands, bathing the afflicted woman in its healing warmth. Together, we toiled. My words of power clashed with the curse, like waves crashing against rocks, slowly wearing it down.

Yet, the curse fought back. It was a tenacious foe, full of malice and wrath. It lashed out, trying to disrupt my concentration, to weaken my resolve. It fed on fear, on desperation. But I wouldn't allow it to feed on ours.

For the first time in a long while, I found myself struggling. But I was not alone in this fight. I had the Srynn. I had to trust in her abilities, in her strength. In the strength of a people that had survived against all odds.

Our resolve did not waver. The Srynn's healing magic flowed constantly, a life-giving stream that fought against the curse's tide. Despite the grimness of the situation, a sense of camaraderie filled the room. The battle raged on for what felt like hours, but we did not yield.

With a final, resounding chant, I summoned all my remaining energy. The air in the room seemed to hum with power, the magic tangible. I saw the curse waver, its grip falter. And then, it was yanked free, a dark, malicious smoke that curled and writhed in the air. I quickly trapped it within a containment crystal, sealing it away.

The room fell silent, save for the woman's steady breathing. The curse was lifted. The woman was free. The Srynn and I, drenched in sweat, exchanged exhausted but triumphant smiles. We had won, against a formidable foe, against grim odds.

In that moment, I understood the true strength of the Srynn people. They had survived, not out of luck, but because of their unwavering resolve, their healing hearts.

As I looked around the room, the young fisherman on his knees beside his mother's bed, tears of relief streaming down his face, I knew that the fight, the struggle, had been worth it. We had not just defeated a curse, but we had restored hope.

With the task completed, I felt a wave of exhaustion wash over me. Yet, there was also satisfaction. A feeling of fulfillment. For today, in this icy town, against a formidable curse, we had won. And we would continue to fight, continue to survive, just like the Srynn.

Chapter 34

The chill of the icy morning bit into my bones as I stepped out of the old house. I glanced back one last time, seeing the silhouette of the Srynn healer and the young fisherman behind the frosted glass. Their relief was palpable, even from outside. With a sigh of satisfaction, I prepared to continue on my journey.

Just as I was about to delve into the winding lanes of the town, a voice called out to me. I turned to see the young fisherman, Alfred, rushing towards me. His face was flushed, not just from the cold, but from a sense of urgency and determination.

"You said you need to cross the Dreadful Expanse, to get to the Frozen Continent, right?" Alfred panted, catching his breath.

"Yes, that's right," I replied, curious about where this was going.

"I'll take you there," he stated, his tone leaving no room for argument.

I stared at him in surprise, then shook my head. "You don't owe me anything, Alfred," I said. "I didn't help your mother for a favour or reward. It was simply the right thing to do."

His eyes were sincere, reflecting the morning light in a way that was both earnest and resolute. "I know that," he said. "And that's exactly why I want to help. You saved my mother's life. I can't ever repay that. But this... this is something I can do."

I studied him for a moment. There was a kind of bravery in his eyes that I hadn't noticed before, a spark of determination. It was the kind of look that people wear when they are ready to face the world, come what may.

"But the Dreadful Expanse isn't called dreadful for nothing," I cautioned, testing his resolve. "Are you sure you're up for it?"

Alfred merely nodded, his gaze unwavering. "I think it's time for a little adventure," he replied with a small smile. "Besides, my mother will be safe now, thanks to you. I think I can afford to be away for a while."

His words brought a smile to my face. It seemed that the young fisherman was not as timid as he appeared.

"I won't forget this, Alfred," I said, extending my hand towards him. He took it, his grip firm and confident. The pact was sealed, an unspoken promise to aid each other in the trials that were sure to come.

Alfred blushed, his fair cheeks turning a bright shade of red against the cold morning. "Likewise," he responded. The morning sun reflected off the icy ground, casting an ethereal glow around us. It felt like the beginning of a new chapter, a new adventure.

And with that, we set off, back to the heart of the fishing town. As the sun began its ascent into the clear, blue sky, we prepared for the journey that lay ahead. To the Dreadful Expanse, to the Frozen Continent. To the unknown.

Chapter 35

The small fishing boat rocked gently in the icy harbour, its wooden structure creaking in the frosty wind. Alfred and I worked side by side, hauling our supplies aboard. There was a certain energy in the air that morning, a mix of anticipation, fear, and excitement.

"So," Alfred started, his voice barely audible over the wind, "I've been wondering about something."

"Ask away," I replied, my hands busy securing a sturdy rope around a barrel of preserved food.

He hesitated for a moment, then spoke, "You're a mage, right? Why can't you just... I don't know, teleport yourself there?" He gestured vaguely towards the open sea, the distant, mythical land of the Frozen Continent still invisible to the naked eye.

I chuckled at the thought. "I wish it were that simple," I said. "But it's not. First, the distance is too far, and my mana can't support that. And then, there's the small issue of not knowing what the place looks like."

Alfred gave me a puzzled look, "You need to know what a place looks like to teleport there?"

"Yes," I replied, "the process requires visualizing the destination. Without a clear image, the teleportation spell could go awry."

"I see," Alfred nodded, processing the information. "And what if you tried anyway?"

I shrugged, "I suppose I could end up in the middle of the sea, and then I'd either freeze to death, drown, or both."

We looked at each other for a moment, before breaking into laughter, the absurdity of the situation punctuating the seriousness of our quest.

Legend of the Ice Demon

"Doesn't sound like the best plan," Alfred remarked, chuckling. "I think I prefer the boat."

The air between us relaxed, the tension easing into a comfortable camaraderie. I found myself grateful for his company; the road ahead seemed less daunting with someone else by my side.

I decided to turn the tables, "What about you? What do you think of those legends about sea serpents in the Dreadful Expanse?"

His expression turned serious, "Well, I guess we're about to find out, aren't we?"

Once again, our laughter echoed through the morning air, a shared joke at the expense of our impending peril. In a way, our shared humour was our shield, helping us face the looming danger with lighter hearts.

Our preparations complete, we stood at the edge of the boat, staring out into the icy expanse before us. The sun had risen higher in the sky, casting long shadows on the wooden planks beneath our feet. As we set out, I couldn't help but feel a strange mix of fear and anticipation. After all, we were headed towards the unknown, towards danger and adventure.

Chapter 36

The boat cut through the icy sea, its bow parting the waves with a sound both soothing and hypnotic. Alfred, with the skills of a seasoned sailor, navigated our vessel through the treacherous expanse. His eyes were alight with determination, yet also a flicker of fear as they scanned the horizon. I found myself studying the old tome, the pages filled with ancient text about Mythical Creatures and Magic Amplification. I tried to keep my focus on the information about the Ice Demon, its existence a fascinating enigma.

However, the silence was punctured by Alfred's voice, "You seem worried." His eyes were on me, the concern evident in his tone.

"I am," I admitted, closing the tome and looking at him. "There's no way to know what awaits us there." I paused before adding, "Antonius must be worried sick."

"Antonius?" Alfred inquired, curiosity piqued.

"My mentor," I clarified, "He's been like a father to me. I ran away from the conservatory against his advice. I hope he forgives me for it." I sighed, the weight of my choices pressing upon me.

Alfred was quiet for a moment. "I lost my father," he confessed, his voice barely audible against the backdrop of crashing waves. "All I have left of him is this boat."

I was taken aback, "I'm sorry, Alfred. What happened?"

"I don't know," he shrugged, trying to mask the pain in his eyes. "He went out to sea one day and never returned. Some say the sea took him, or maybe it was the sea monsters." He glanced down at his hands. "All I know is that I miss him."

I reached out, placing my hand over his. His skin was soft and cold, yet there was a warmth to him that was comforting. "I'm sorry," I said softly, looking into his eyes. "But if it's worth anything, I think your father would be very proud of the man you've become. Taking care of your mother the way you have."

Alfred blushed, a rosy hue spreading across his cheeks. He stuttered a quick, "Thank you," before pulling his hand away. I noticed the redness of his lips, so prominent against his pale skin. It was a detail I had overlooked before.

"I should get back to the wheel," Alfred said, standing abruptly. His voice sounded a bit shaky, and I couldn't help but wonder if our conversation had affected him as much as it had me.

"Right," I replied, watching him return to his duties

Chapter 37

The rhythm of the waves against the boat's hull, the gentle swaying, the lonely whispers of the sea breeze—they should've lulled me to sleep. Yet, I found myself wide awake in the narrow bunk bed, the glowing words of the ancient tome dancing in front of me, their illumination faintly lighting up the dark cabin.

Joel Poe

The sound of soft footsteps broke the serenity of the night. I didn't have to look up to know who it was. I could feel Alfred's presence, a warmth that cut through the icy cold of the cabin. He hovered near the door, his thin silhouette framed by the dim glow seeping in from outside.

Our eyes met. Words weren't needed. This was a conversation that transcended the confines of language.

Closing the tome, I placed it on the small shelf by the bunk. As if heeding an unspoken call, Alfred moved closer. He was a beacon of warmth in the otherwise frosty cabin. I made room on my bunk, giving him a silent invitation. A slight hesitation, then he was next to me, pulling down his pants and lying upside down on the bed. A dance of shadows played on his face as he looked up at me.

Carefully, I positioned myself over him, taking complete control of his soft and vulnerable shape, my heart hammering in my chest. This was unfamiliar territory, yet it felt as natural as casting a spell. I felt the strong pulse in his neck as I held him down gently, his eyes wide and looking up at me. His lower spine curled and quivered, yearning for my touch, an intimate plea shaped in the silhouette of his body, begging me to claim him as my own.

There we were, two souls in the quiet darkness of the cabin, riding the waves of the unspoken, the tension palpable, the moment stretched like the infinite expanse of the sea surrounding us. I didn't know what tomorrow would bring, what dangers we would face, but in that moment, everything else faded away.

Chapter 38

The ship's violent shudder and a deafening crash pulled me from the quiet sanctuary of dreams. The tranquil sea was a mere memory as I found myself flung out of bed. Alfred, who had been soundly asleep on my chest, looked around in bewilderment. Pulling on our clothes with an urgency only fear can inspire, we stumbled out into the chaos.

There, towering over our small fishing vessel, a gigantic sea serpent rose from the depths of the sea, its enormous body writhing, gleaming in the pale light. It hissed menacingly, baring its monstrous fangs. A feeling of dread washed over me, not unlike the dreadful expanse itself. It was straight out of the myths and legends, a beast of unimaginable power.

"Alfred, get back inside," I shouted over the deafening roar of the beast, trying to force authority into my voice.

He shook his head stubbornly, his jaw set. "I won't leave you alone."

"Alfred," I bellowed in the sternest tone I could muster. "There's nothing you can do here. This beast is beyond both of us, and I won't let you get hurt."

His eyes reflected a mix of fear and determination, but he finally relented, retreating back into the cabin with one last worried glance. As the door closed behind him, I squared off against the sea serpent, its colossal size making the ship feel like a tiny raft.

My HP and mana bars appeared before my eyes, a visual reminder of the immense challenge before me. Calling on my years of study and training, I prepared to fight the beast, relying on my wind and shadow spells, quickly swapping between defense and offense. The serpent lunged, its enormous body crashing against the ship, threatening to capsize us. I responded with wind shields and frost barriers, darting around the boat, my ice shard spell peppering its hide.

The battle raged, the serpent's roars echoing in the night, intermingled with the incantations that ripped from my throat. With each strike, the creature's HP slowly dwindled, but so did mine. Our health and mana bars fluctuated wildly, the tension as palpable as the deadly dance we were locked in.

The fight reached its crescendo as I invoked a spell I had learned in the fog-shrouded mountains – Arcane Wind Blade. The spell materialized a swirling sword of wind, cutting through the air with deadly precision. The blade swept down on the serpent's thick neck, cleaving through scales and sinew. With a final, agonized roar, the sea serpent's head was separated from its body, and the colossal form crashed into the sea.

Breathing heavily, my heart pounding, I watched as my level shot up, the sea serpent's defeat granting me a massive EXP boost.

The door to the cabin creaked open, and Alfred stepped out. His eyes were wide, taking in the sight of the decapitated beast. He looked at me, a multitude of emotions flickering across his face. Then, he crossed the deck in a few strides and kissed me.

Joel Poe

Chapter 39

Our passionate embrace was broken by an icy gust of wind, a chill that spread through my body despite the warmth that lingered from Alfred's touch. The thick clouds parted, revealing a landmass in the distance, a landscape of frost and snow, the air around it shimmering with cold. I knew, in that moment, that we had reached our destination—the forsaken continent. A place lost to the ages, shrouded in myth and mystery, where sunlight could not pierce through the deep, cold haze that hung over it.

As I prepared to leave the relative safety of the boat and venture into the perilous unknown, Alfred moved to join me. I stopped him, my hand firm on his chest.

"No, Alfred," I said, my tone stern but gentle. "This is something I must do alone."

His brows furrowed, and he looked at me, hurt flashing in his eyes. "You're just trying to get rid of me," he accused. "Don't worry, I won't tell anyone about...us. If that's what you're worried about."

I let out a chuckle, shaking my head. "It's not that. I don't care what people think or say. I don't give a damn about that. But I do care about you, Alfred. I don't want you to get hurt. Your mother needs you. This place—it's full of terrors that we can't even imagine."

I saw the reluctant understanding in his eyes, his jaw working as he battled with his own concerns and the stark reality of my words.

"Your mother," I continued, "has already lost your father. She can't afford to lose you too."

He pulled me into an embrace, his grip tight as he tried to convey his fear, his reluctance, his worry, in that single touch.

"I'll be back in three days," he promised, pulling back to look me in the eyes. "If you're not waiting here, I will go in after you."

"No," I said firmly, my grip on his arms tightening. "If you don't see me, it's because I didn't make it. You're to go back to safety. Promise me, Alfred."

His eyes searched mine, as if looking for an alternative to the bleak picture I had painted. Finding none, he nodded. He pulled me in for a final kiss, a touch that was both sweet and sorrowful.

"And Alfred," I added, pulling back slightly to look into his eyes. "I'm not ashamed of what happened. I just want you to know that."

He blushed but gave me a small, uncertain smile. "Maybe when you return we can..."

I interrupted him with a shake of my head. "Let's not get ahead of ourselves. The odds aren't great for me making it back."

We laughed then, an awkward sound that echoed against the quiet of the desolate land that stretched before me.

"I'll see you soon," Alfred said, his voice barely above a whisper.

"I hope so," I replied, letting go of his hand as I turned toward the icy wasteland that awaited me.

Chapter 40

It was unlike anything I had ever experienced. The cold of the forsaken continent, an uninhabitable, barren wilderness, bit into my very bones with an unimaginable ferocity. The howling winds were unrelenting, tearing at my cloak and skin with a fierce, icy grip. But I steeled myself against it all, a lone silhouette against the vast, icy wilderness. With each laborious step into the frozen expanse, my thoughts inevitably drifted back to Alfred, leaving me with an odd mix of worry and hope. I found myself silently praying for his safe return to the small fishing town.

In the midst of my weary trek, a soft, cool light broke through my reverie. The pulsing glow emanated from my floating codex, indicating a notification. "Achievement Unlocked: Discovering Land of the Demon." The message on my Heads-Up Display (HUD) filled me with a sense of unease. The ominous title felt like an ill-omen, the foreboding shadow of a yet unseen terror. But this was no time for fear - I was here for a reason.

As I trudged deeper into the hostile terrain, a curious sight caught my eye.

Half-buried under blankets of snow were the remnants of what appeared to be ancient ruins. The structures were largely dilapidated, the weather and time having taken their toll. However, they bore a ghostly reminiscence of a once-thriving civilization, their origin, and purpose as mysterious as the land they resided in.

Intrigued, I prompted the codex for information on any civilizations that might have existed on this desolate continent. It responded, rather disconcertingly, with "Information Unavailable for Public Disclosure." This unexpected response left me baffled. It was the second time the codex had withheld information, information that Antonius himself must have deemed unnecessary for my magical studies. But why?

I found myself staring at the ancient structures, a sense of fascination replacing my initial confusion. Despite their deteriorated state, there was an inherent complexity to the architectural design that was strangely captivating. The structures bore an uncanny combination of artistic grandeur and engineering marvel, a signature of an advanced civilization. The peculiar design did not resemble the architectural styles of any Aellorian civilizations I was aware of.

These thoughts brought forth a barrage of questions. Was there an entire civilization wiped out from memory and history? If so, who were they, and why was their existence hidden? The prospect of an ancient, forgotten civilization filled me with an inquisitive excitement. But it also came with a lingering feeling of apprehension. Was this the same fear Antonius had sought to protect me from by withholding such information?

With nightfall rapidly closing in, I knew I needed to seek shelter. Despite the enigma surrounding them, the ruins provided me with the only available refuge in this frozen wasteland. I decided to set up camp amidst these strange structures, hoping their ancient walls would offer some protection against the biting cold. I couldn't shake off a sense of foreboding as I settled in, the ruins and their secrets seeming to echo in the silence of the night.

As I huddled into my makeshift shelter, I couldn't help but ponder the mysteries that lay ahead. The ancient ruins, the inexplicable codex response, the achievement warning; they all hinted at a dangerous journey. But for now, my immediate concern was survival in this frigid land.

Throughout it all, one thought remained clear. I was a lone mage in a perilous, unknown land teeming with secrets and potential threats. But I had a mission. And no matter the odds, I was determined to see it through. With that conviction in my heart, I steeled myself against the night, the echoes of the ancient ruins my only company in the desolate cold of the forsaken continent.

Chapter 41

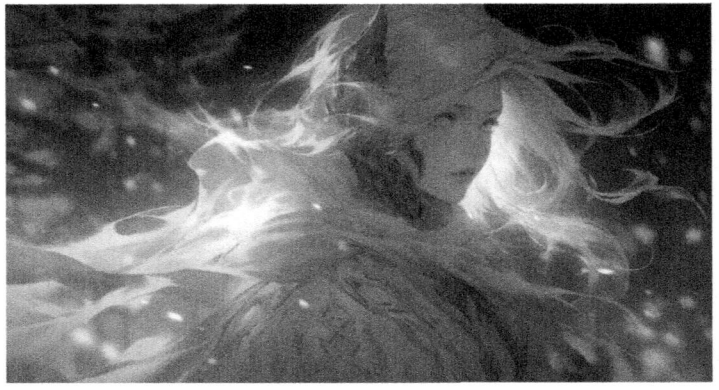

The night had settled in when I was roused from my restless slumber by an eerie wailing. The sound echoed through the icy wilderness, making the hair on the back of my neck stand up. It was the mournful cry of a banshee, a spirit from the netherworld, and it seemed to be beckoning me. I found myself drawn towards it, lured by an inexplicable force as I ventured deeper into the ice forest.

The stark moonlight cast long shadows on the snow-laden forest floor as I pressed on. Each echoing wail was a siren's call, guiding me towards a solitary fountain nestled in the heart of the forest. A spectral figure floated next to the fountain, her wailing filling the night air. As I approached, I could see her clearer - a banshee with spectral features, but the melancholy in her eyes seemed all too human.

Fearing not her apparition but the pain in her eyes, I lowered my magical staff, signaling my peaceful intentions. She halted her haunting cries, her gaze affixed upon me. The ethereal figure moved her lips, her voice a haunting echo in the still forest, "Thou art in pursuit of the white demon, art thou not?"

Taken aback, I asked, "How do you know of my quest?". She replied with a melancholic note to her voice, "I hath seen thy coming, waited for thee for a hundred winters."

Intrigued, I pressed, "What happened to you? Why is your spirit tormented? Why are you chained to the material realm and unable to find peace in the unseen?" My questions lingered in the frosty air as I looked upon the tortured apparition.

She gestured towards the fountain and said, "All thy answers shall thee find in the reflection of this fountain." Her spectral figure became more transparent as she moved back, her form almost blending with the moonlit night.

As I neared the fountain, the banshee appeared not as a fearsome apparition but a maiden of otherworldly beauty. Her ethereal form was adorned with flowing white hair and sorrowful blue eyes. I leaned over the fountain, its serene water reflecting the moon and stars. As my gaze met the reflection, a surge of magical energy rippled through me, and I was pulled into the depths of the water.

Suddenly, I was no longer standing in the frosty wilderness of the forsaken continent. I was swept off my feet, carried by a torrent of memories and echoes from the past, hurtling through time and space, back to a time two millennia ago. The icy fountain and the wailing banshee disappeared into the background as the world around me morphed, and I was flung into the mysteries of the past.

Chapter 42

Two millennia ago, the world was a different place. A proud civilization thrived on this icy landscape, living in harmony and balance with nature. Majestic temples, buildings of exquisite architecture, intricate ice sculptures, and grand palaces stood tall and magnificent, all of them shining in the endless snow. They were mages, all of them, masters of ice and arcane magic. Their white hair, as pristine as the snow around them, flowed freely, while their blue eyes held the essence of the cold, clear sky. They bore a striking resemblance to me, so much so that it was unsettling.

Legend of the Ice Demon

Through these visions, I watched their lives, their practices, their culture. They were a peaceful society, their magical knowledge far surpassing any I had seen. They lived in harmony with their land, drawing strength from the icy tundra, the winter winds, and the endless snow. Their magic was woven into their daily lives, as natural as breathing.

And then, the day of reckoning arrived. The Ice Demon descended upon the land, its icy breath snuffing out life wherever it went. The mages, peaceful as they were, rose to the challenge. The war that ensued was one of epic proportions, a struggle for survival that lasted for five centuries. They fought with all their might, their lands shattering under the force of the demon's fury and their own desperate counterattacks.

The demon was insatiable, desiring to consume all life and magic in its path. It was chaos incarnate, leaving a trail of death and destruction in its wake. But the mages of the frost didn't falter. They held their ground, their bravery shining through the despair.

Their king, a mage of unparalleled power, in a final desperate attempt, binded the Ice Demon to this land. With a sealing spell of such magnitude, he ensured that the demon would never be able to leave this continent and wreak havoc on the rest of the world. But such a spell came at a great cost. The king's life force was drained, his soul consumed by the spell. His death was not in vain, however. His sacrifice bought the world time, and he condemned the Ice Demon to an eternal prison.

But many of his people were less fortunate. Their souls were trapped in the icy tundra, cursed to wander for eternity until their heir, the heir of the blue-eyed mages, would return to free them and finally slay the Ice Demon.

I came out of the vision, my head spinning from the onslaught of information. It was as if I had lived through those events myself. The history of this forgotten civilization was mine now, imprinted in my mind.

The banshee, her spectral figure starting to fade, waited for my response. I turned to her, her sorrowful blue eyes mirroring my own, "Who am I to you?" I asked. Her answer was a whisper, fading into the night, "Deliver us, Kolos". As her voice disappeared, I was left alone once more, the revelations of the past heavy on my mind. The vision had shown me a daunting task, a responsibility inherited from centuries ago. It was my task now, to free these trapped souls and to put an end to the Ice Demon.

Chapter 43

Shaken to my core, I stood alone in the unforgiving cold of the forsaken continent. The night sky, filled with countless twinkling stars, only accentuated the solitude I felt. The vision that the Banshee had shown me was relentless in my mind, playing again and again like a song stuck on repeat.

These people, these mages of ice and arcane, could they be my ancestors? I had always been an outsider, never fitting in, never belonging. But in the vision, I saw a civilization that held an uncanny resemblance to me. Was this my true heritage, my lineage?

And what about this prophecy? Was I the heir it spoke of? Was I the one destined to save these trapped souls and bring down the Ice Demon? Was this quest that I found myself on not a mere coincidence but a path I was meant to walk?

This train of thought inevitably led me to the question of my parents. I had never known them. Who were they? Did they know of this prophecy, of this destiny that seemed to befall me? I was just an orphan, a former slave, a mage apprentice. How could I be the heir, the savior, that this ancient civilization was waiting for?

My mind was a whirlwind of questions, thoughts, doubts. I felt a sinking feeling in my chest, the weight of what I had learned pressing down on me. I didn't know what to do, where to start. But one thing was clear. I needed answers, I needed guidance.

Summoning an orb of communication, a sphere of magical energy that allowed for long-distance interaction, I reached out to the one person who might have answers. The orb flickered to life, and the image of Antonius, my mentor and father-figure, formed within it.

"Kolos," Antonius's voice echoed out, filled with concern, "Are you alright? Where are you? You need to come back to the conservatory at once."

I took a deep breath, trying to calm the storm raging within me, and replied, "You knew, didn't you? You knew all along."

Antonius paused, his eyes narrowing as he scrutinized me, taking in my surroundings. He knew where I was. I could see it in his eyes. He realized I was in the forsaken continent.

"Kolos," He sighed, his voice heavy with regret and worry, "I did not tell you because I wanted to protect you. I can see now that you've made it to the forsaken land. I can see the questions in your eyes, and son, I wish I had prepared you better. But whatever you do, do not face the demon alone. It is exactly what it wants."

His words were a plea, a warning, and a testament to his fear. But I couldn't back down now. Not when I was this close to the truth, not when I was possibly the only hope for the trapped souls of this land.

"The Paragons and I will channel a teleportation spell strong enough to breach the gap and reach you. Please, son, stay where you are. Don't do anything rash."

But his words fell on deaf ears. I had made up my mind. I couldn't wait. Not when there was so much at stake.

"I can't do that," I said, my voice determined, resolute. "I have to see this through."

With that, I closed the magical orb, severing the connection. I was alone once again in the heart of the forsaken continent, the weight of my destiny hanging over me like the cold, unforgiving sky above. I didn't know what lay ahead, didn't know if I could truly defeat the Ice Demon, but I was determined to try. For the trapped souls of the ancient civilization, for my possible ancestors, for myself.

Chapter 44

Darkness prevailed over the icy landscape, only interrupted by the occasional luminescence of my staff, as it cast eerie shadows against the ancient ruins. The bitter cold gnawed at my skin relentlessly, reminding me with every biting gust of wind of the harsh, inhospitable world I had ventured into. Despite the perilous environment, I felt a strange sense of connection with this place, a surreal familiarity that tugged at the strings of my heart.

I was exhausted, emotionally drained by the revelations of the past few days. Learning that I was the heir to a forgotten civilization, destined to confront an ancient demon, had cast me into a whirlwind of confusion and fear. But above it all, an unyielding determination flared within me. I was destined to face this demon, and I would not back down.

As I stood amidst the ruins, I could feel a ripple of energy emanating from them, a faint resonance with my own magic. It was as if the souls of my ancestors were whispering to me, reaching out across the centuries. I was the last of their line, their final hope.

I raised my staff high into the cold night air, closing my eyes and focusing on the subtle vibrations of magic around me. I called upon the spirits of my ancestors, my voice echoing against the skeletal remains of their city. "Show me the way!" I cried out, my voice carrying in the wind. "Show me where the demon dwells!"

For a moment, there was nothing but the icy silence of the desolate wasteland. Then, in a wave of spectral energy, a multitude of spirits materialized before me. They were ethereal figures, shimmering with a cold, blue light, their eyes mirrors of my own. Their sorrowful expressions bore the weight of centuries of torment.

I could feel them passing through me, their essence seeping into my being. An immense rush of energy surged through my body, like a current of icy water, and my vision blurred. Suddenly, I was thrust into the past, my mind consumed by the memory of the ancient king.

The vision was crystal clear, as if I were living it myself. I stood before a towering demon, an abhorrent beast of ice and darkness, its presence radiating an intense, bone-chilling cold. I could feel the king's determination, his will to protect his people, as he wielded a staff much like my own.

I watched as the king cast a spell of binding, a surge of power unlike anything I had ever felt. The demon roared, its piercing shriek echoing through the mountains, as it was sealed within the heart of the icy range. As the king collapsed, his life force spent, I could feel a deep sense of satisfaction mixed with profound sadness within him.

Legend of the Ice Demon

I was brought back to the present abruptly, the spirits of my ancestors fading away like wisps of smoke. I stood there, alone amidst the ruins, the echo of their guidance lingering in my mind. The taste of their memories was bitter in my mouth, but the path they had shown me was clear.

I looked towards the towering mountains in the distance, their peaks veiled in the perpetual haze. The demon was there, bound in its icy prison. The sense of dread that loomed over me was potent, a cold hand gripping my heart. But there was a fire within me that it could not quench, a burning resolve that had been ignited by the knowledge of my heritage.

"I know where you are," I murmured, my voice barely more than a whisper carried away by the frigid wind. My words echoed into the darkness, a promise to the ancient evil that lay hidden within the mountains.

I began my journey towards the heart of the forsaken continent. Each step was a challenge, a battle against the unyielding cold and the weight of my destiny. But I would not falter, not now. I was Kolos, the heir to the Blue-Eyed Mages, the last beacon of hope for a civilization lost in time. I was their deliverer, their chosen one, and I would confront the Ice Demon.

I was no longer a slave, an apprentice, or even a mage. I was a warrior on a sacred quest, and I would face whatever trials lay ahead. And when I finally stood before the demon, I would not be alone. I would carry the spirits of my ancestors with me, their hopes and dreams fuelling my resolve.

With each step towards my destiny, I left behind a piece of the boy I once was, embracing the man I was meant to be. The path was treacherous, fraught with dangers and uncertainty. But I was ready. I had found my purpose.

As the echoes of my past and the whispers of my future intertwined, I forged onwards, into the heart of the forsaken land, towards the beast that lay in wait. For I knew where the demon was. And I was coming for it.

Chapter 45

It was a trek that felt like an eternity, each step drawing me deeper into the ominous presence that marked the Ice Demon's prison. The very air seemed saturated with an eerie darkness, a malicious energy that seemed to pulsate and seethe around me. Yet beneath the layers of fear and trepidation, I could feel a strong resonance, a powerful surge of magic that only confirmed what my visions had shown.

Arriving at the heart of this ancient battleground, I could see the remnants of the fight that had taken place here centuries ago. The icy terrain was scarred, pitted, and marred, reflecting the intensity of the magical duel between the ancient king and the demon. It was a place imbued with history, a past painted in shades of valor and sacrifice.

As I moved deeper into the location, the air seemed to crackle with an unseen power. I could sense the demon's essence—its malice, its hunger, and its overwhelming strength. The intensity of it all hit me like a wave, each pulsation causing my heart to race and my skin to prickle with anticipation.

Suddenly, I was bombarded with flashes of memories that were not mine. Visions of a fearsome duel, of spells clashing against the roars of the demon, and of a king giving his all to protect his people. The memories were fragmented and erratic, like shards of a shattered mirror, but each piece painted a picture of a battle of epic proportions.

My breaths came out in ragged gasps, the memories leaving me winded. Yet, I found myself shouting into the abyss. "Show yourself!" My voice rang out, echoing off the icy walls of the mountains, daring the beast to face me.

The response I received was a laugh, a sound that rippled through the air, carrying a dark delight that sent shivers down my spine. The mocking amusement in it was palpable, the demon reveling in the audacity of my challenge.

Emboldened, I shouted again, my words ringing loud and clear in the chilling silence. "Coward! Come out and face me!" I was met with silence, the eeriness of it only fueling my determination.

Then, a voice echoed through the desolate landscape. It was a chilling sound, guttural and malicious, dripping with sinister delight. "So, the prodigal son has come to die, at last," the demon taunted. Its words, laced with scorn and mockery, served as a chilling reminder of the beast's immense power.

The air around me seemed to drop in temperature drastically, the icy cold gnawing into my very bones. Then, a rumbling sound echoed, growing louder and more pronounced. It was the sound of steps, massive and powerful, each one making the icy ground beneath my feet quake.

Through the foggy haze, a massive silhouette began to materialize. It was a figure of colossal size, its mere presence dominating the landscape. As it stepped into full view, I found myself staring at the Ice Demon.

Legend of the Ice Demon

It was a sight to behold, a terrifying, awe-inspiring creature forged from ice and darkness. Its sheer size dwarfed the surrounding mountains, its form seemingly woven from the very essence of the cold and desolation that encompassed the forsaken continent.

My heart pounded in my chest, a rhythm of fear and resolve. I was looking into the face of my destiny, the creature I had been born to fight. It was a chilling realization, one that filled me with a sense of dread. Yet, beneath it all, a flame of determination burned bright.

Joel Poe

With my staff clenched in my hand
and the spirits of my ancestors
guiding me, I stood before the demon.

Chapter 46

With the monstrous Ice Demon looming over me, its frosty breath snaking out in the frigid air, I braced myself. The creature was a behemoth, an incarnation of frost and fury, its icy gaze full of malevolent amusement.

"Such audacity thou showest," its words reverberated around me, as cold and biting as the relentless wind. "The final descendent of the Blue Mages has come to meet his demise. Today, thy bloodline shall cease."

Fury simmered in me, but I clung onto the steadfast calm radiating from the spirits of my forebears. They were with me, their wisdom whispered in my ears and their strength bolstered my resolve.

"Indeed, I am the last of the Blue Mages," I asserted, my voice resonating against the barren landscape. "But remember, monster, my people lived with dignity and valour. They defied you for centuries. Now, it's my turn."

A thunderous, mirthless laughter tumbled from the beast. "Valor? Dignity? Mere words, they art. Shalt thy words shield thee, boy? Or wilt they perish with thee?"

"Words hold power you fail to understand," I shot back, bolstered by the spiritual chorus of my ancestors. Their whispers intensified, a symphony of resilience and wisdom within my mind. "Words shape destinies. Words can be as powerful as the mightiest of spells."

The demon sneered, its cruel, twisted mouth a stark contrast to the delicate snowflakes swirling around us. "Art thou prepared to stake thy life on such a belief, young mage?"

I drew myself to my full height, meeting the demon's icy gaze with unwavering determination. I felt the spirits of my lineage rallying behind me, their voices a steady drumbeat in my mind.

"Prepare yourself, Demon of Ice," I declared, my words echoing out into the frozen expanse. "Today, you face the last of the Blue Mages. Today, you face your end."

With that, the icy ground beneath me cracked with a thunderous roar, a brilliant white light enveloping everything. Darkness fell as a deafening silence consumed the surroundings.

The final confrontation had begun.

Legend of the Ice Demon

Joel Poe

Epilogue

Information Available for Public Disclosure

Game Lore:

In the hallowed chronicles of olden times, echoes of a dire apparition seep into the world's marrow, an ancient specter born of frost and shadows, the Ice Demon. 'Tis a ghoul of unfathomable prowess, woven from the earliest fabric of the cosmos itself. Its lore remains as elusive as the gossamer tendrils of a dream, ensnared only in the cobwebs of ancient ballads and cryptic parchments long discarded as fanciful tales. Among the humble hearthfolk, it is whispered in hushed voices as the

Legend of the Ice Demon

Defiler, a curse in the wind, a chill in the bone.

The sylvan kin, the eternal elves, shrouded in the silver glow of the moon and the wisdom of countless summers, they name it Ithur. Legend paints this creature with myriad brushes, each tale churning a different beast. At times, it appears as a serpent pure as the driven snow, its scales shimmering with a cold, otherworldly glow. Elsewhere, it assumes the guise of a spectral bull, its form a grotesque parody of sacred, a blasphemy in white. Yet in other fables, it stands as a colossal chimera, a terror birthed from ice and death.

The learned scholars, the quiet custodians of ancient lore, postulate the discrepancies in its depiction to be testament to the Demon's transformative might. Indeed, it weaves its essence like a frostbitten tapestry, becoming the behemoth, the serpent, the chimera – always shifting, always elusive.

As one delves deeper into the genesis, the Ice Demon takes a hallowed seat in the creation mythos. An entity primordial, an antithesis born to counter the eternal flame of the Phoenix. As the Phoenix burns with life, the Ice Demon chills with oblivion. They are two sides of the same coin, light and darkness, heat and cold, existence and void, the equilibrium of the universe hinged upon their cosmic dance. They are bound in an eternal standoff, each one keeping the other tethered, a balance as ancient as time itself.

Legend of the Ice Demon

Class: Primordial
Level: Unspecified
Element/Affinity: Ice, Shadow
Unique Affinity: Shapeshifter
HP: ∞
Mana: ∞

Joel Poe

To Be Continued...

Thank you for reading.

To receive emails regarding upcoming book deals, free book giveaways and updates on release dates sign up at:

https://joelpoe.com/contact/

*Consider sharing your experience on **Amazon** and **Goodreads**. Reviews and ratings from readers like you help new readers find this book.*

Plus, it is what helps me measure your interest in this particular story, to decide whether I should or shouldn't write more sequels.

Till next time,

Joel Poe

Printed in Great Britain
by Amazon